The
Dark Room

Cindy L. Freeman

HighTide
Publications, Inc.

For permission requests, write to the publisher, addressed "Attention: Permissions Coordinator," at the address below.

High Tide Publications, Inc.
1000 Bland Point Road
Deltaville, Virginia 23043
www.HighTidePublications.com

Edited by: Narielle Living (NarielleLiving@gmail.com)
Cover by: Firebelliedfrog@gmail.com

Publisher's Note: This is a work of fiction. Names, characters, businesses, places, events and incidents are either the products of the author's imagination or used in a fictitious manner. Locales and public names are used for atmospheric purposes. Any resemblance to actual persons, living or dead, or to businesses, companies, institutions, actual events or locales is purely coincidental.

First Edition: March 30, 2017
BISAC: FIC031080 FICTION / Thrillers / Psychological
Printed in the United States of America
ISBN: 978-1945990-02-1

Foreward

By Beverly Peterson, PhD

In graduate school, I researched the ways women in America in the mid-19th century used fiction to participate in political discussions on the subject of slavery. One woman succeeded beyond anything before or since, and that was Harriet Beecher Stowe with *Uncle Tom's Cabin*. But most of these women's novels were clumsy attempts to meld information and persuasion into a readable narrative with believable characters. Their dialog became "speechifying." In *The Dark Room*, Cindy Freeman has seamlessly joined a suspenseful, touching plot with an informative presentation of facts about what happens in abusive relationships and why. Her dialog is realistic. Her characters live. They drive the novel because it is impossible not to care about them, grieve for what they have endured, and rejoice when they prevail.

Because of the author's thorough research, the realistic details about even minor elements of the story contribute to the overall believability of the plot. The most important research—and the most important social contribution this book makes—concerns abuse. Women reading this novel will learn what kinds of motives drive abusers and how they manipulate their victims, making the victims feel that they deserve the abuse they get. We see how abusers isolate their victims from a supportive community. Then the abuser destroys his victim's self-esteem, making it impossible for her to effectively defend herself. Give her a child to protect and limit her access to money and transportation, and the question changes from "Why didn't she leave?" to "How on earth did she finally break away?"

I particularly appreciate the way *The Dark Room* shows how a person can effectively help a woman who is being abused. In the novel, Edith's instincts take her far in allowing her to see what is going on and to realize that she must proceed cautiously or else risk scaring Stella or even putting her at greater risk from Hank's fury. What she learns from Mike about helping a victim of abuse contributes to her effectiveness and educates us readers.

The settings are believable, too. I can see Edith's restaurant, Hank's horrible house with the abominable dark room, the room in the women's prison where prisoners receive visitors, the shelter with its public rooms and cheery bedrooms, the hospital where Jodie is taken for treatment, and—on a happier note—the French restaurant where Edith and Mike have their special table and outdoor bench.

Creating Mike, the police sergeant, was a smart move. He provides the perspective of law enforcement on dealing with abusers and their victims. He is a perfect partner for Edith. His vulnerability, strength, and decency provide a counterbalance to the abusers in the story, chief among them, of course, being Hank. Mike's presence ensures that no one can read this book and think it is just male-bashing.

Back to Hank. Reluctantly. The way Cindy Freeman explains his behavior without condoning it is a remarkable balancing act. What Stella learns in the shelter about forgiving and forgetting is relevant for many situations. While Hank is a deeply flawed person, he is more complex than a horror-movie villain. He gets the punishment he deserves, leaving the reader feeling that justice prevails when good people, people like Edith and Mike, go out of their way to make it prevail.

The characters' back stories are integrated right into the various narratives. Through them, we learn about Edith's first marriage, the loss of her child, and her faith. We learn that her experiences and her religion are terrific sources of strength for her, and the fact that she finds happiness and love helps to convey the sense that goodness and strength will be rewarded.

As a former English professor, I loved watching Stella work on her speech as part of her self-improvement, and I applauded Amy's success in completing her degree while imprisoned. My husband, Joe Galano, who has worked in the field of child abuse prevention, agrees that although this book is a work of fiction, it has the potential to help and to heal. Together, we intend to donate multiple copies of *The Dark Room* to our local battered women's shelter.

Chapter 1

Jodie

I think I had a name when I first got born. But I don't have a name now. At least they don't call me anything. They don't talk to me much at all. So, I don't talk to them neither. They think I can't talk but I learned how by listening. What else I got to do? Mostly I talk inside my head. I gave myself a name. "Sweetie" I call me. Don't know why. Maybe I heard it on the television box. That's a talking box in the next room. I ain't seen the picture in a long time but I hear it playing all day long. Right before the door slams every morning they turn it loud so nobody can hear me, but I gave up screaming a long time ago because it doesn't make any difference. Just makes Hank mad and hurts my throat.

Whenever Hank or Stella come I try to look through the doorway to the next room, but my eyes are used to being in the dark. The light hurts so I keep 'em partway shut and peek out just a little. I start to see shadows or a chair or light coming in a window. I wish I could sit by that window and feel the sun on my skin. Mostly the woman—Stella—comes. She brings me food or water for my drinking pan. Hank keeps my leg strapped to the bed so I can't stretch but so far. He only comes to make sure I'm being good.

I wasn't always in this here dark room. I remember a pretty-faced woman—or was she a girl? She had long yellow hair like mine but clean. She was sweet, too… sweet and pretty. I think that was about three summers ago. I don't know how old I am, but she's been gone a long time. Maybe I'm six or maybe seven. Anyways, they called her Amy. She went away… didn't say good-bye or anything… just went away and never came back. I think I was happy then, but I can't remember for sure. I think Amy smiled at me and talked to me. Maybe I dreamed it, but I remember she liked me. After Amy left, Hank put me here. At first I screamed and screamed till I couldn't scream no more. Hank came and hit me to make me stop. Finally—I don't know how many times I got hit—I gave up and stopped screaming. I didn't want to get hit anymore and besides I got hungry. Hank said he wouldn't let Stella bring me food till I stopped screaming. I still cry sometimes, but I don't scream anymore.

Stella brings my food but sometimes she forgets or maybe she's hurting too much from Hank beating her. I can always hear her coming because of her cane: shuffle-shuffle-tap, shuffle-shuffle-tap. It taps on the wood floor. I started hiding food under the mattress so I'd have some in case she can't come, but the mice got it and made a hole in my mattress getting to it. Now if Stella forgets to bring food I just chew on my hair and pretend it's food. Then I go to sleep so I can't feel my belly hurting.

Stella don't hit me, but she don't talk to me either. I can tell by her eyes she wants to, except she ain't allowed. I hear Hank telling her not to talk to the "bastard girl." At first I asked her questions like "Where's Amy? Why don't she come back? Why can't I go with Amy?" I told her I was scared to stay in this dark room by myself. She'd look at me with the saddest face, like she wanted to say something. Then she'd look at the floor and shake her head. Mostly she just leaves my food and takes my piss-pot to empty it.

If Hank thinks Stella stays too long or talks to me, he beats me first. Then he hits her and hits her. I can hear her in the next room begging him to stop, but he never stops till all the beatings are out of him. He calls her mean names like "ugly bitch" and "worthless sow". He yells questions she can't answer like, "Why can't you do nothin' right?" and "When are you gonna learn to do as yer told?" I cry when Hank beats Stella, but at least when he's hitting her he ain't hitting me.

Edith

Stella showed up at the restaurant today with more bruises. She tried to cover them with makeup but I could tell they were fresh. I'm sure her husband beats her but I don't know how to help. Once I asked her how she got some new bruises on her arms. She said she tripped over her cane and fell. She couldn't look me in the eyes though. I keep trying to get to know her, but she won't talk any more than she absolutely must. She never mentions anything about her personal life. Stella is a hard worker. She manages to serve the customers and carry heavy trays even with that cane. She's good at remembering orders, and she can handle numerous tables at once without getting the orders mixed up.

When Stella first applied for the server position, I hesitated to hire her. To tell the truth, she looked like a bag lady and sounded ignorant. Now that I know her, I'm ashamed of my initial assessment. I thought she was a lot older than forty-five, but her employment paperwork confirmed her age. It's obvious she has had a hard life. Her face has the wrinkles of a seventy-year-old and her hair is… well, let's just say she doesn't spend any time at the beauty parlor. She told me some story about having polio as a kid, but I'm convinced that no-good husband of hers caused her permanent limp.

Like I said before, at our first meeting I had no intention of hiring Stella, but she convinced me—begged me, really—to give her a chance. On the spot, she showed me how she could balance a tray filled with dishes. I figured the uniform would take care of her sloppy dress, and the required hairnet would tame that gray mop of hers. So, I decided to risk it. I confess Stella has turned out to be a most reliable, hardworking employee. Somehow, she manages to turn on the charm with the customers and they seem to like her. My regulars even ask for her. Stella works straight through her shift from seven a.m. until three-thirty p.m., eating lunch on the run. Before she leaves each afternoon, she makes sure the tables are set and ready for the dinner shift. Then she hobbles to the corner of Second and Main to catch the four o'clock bus. I wish I could pay her more but the recession hit our whole town hard. People here in Hickory don't eat out as often as they used to. Like Lexington, Hickory, North Carolina once had a booming furniture and textile industry, but since most of the actual manufacturing outsourced to Asia, many folks have been left without jobs.

Stella would make more in tips if she worked the dinner shift, but she says she has to get home to cook dinner for her husband. His name is Hank. She doesn't talk about him—and I've never met him—but he must some piece-of-work.

Jodie

One time Stella brought me a picture book. She whispered for me to hide it under my mattress and take it out only after Hank left for work. Even though my window is covered with a thick blanket, I can tell when morning comes because there's a window in the next room where the sun comes in and the light shines under my door—and because I can smell the coffee brewing. Sometimes, if I don't make a sound, Stella leaves my door open a crack. Anyway, I could hardly wait to look at the picture book. I waited till the sun came through the window and I smelled the coffee. Then the front door slammed, meaning Hank left for work.

I lifted the corner of the mattress—the corner that ain't been chewed by mice. I pulled out the book with shiny pages and opened it. It's dark in my room. So, I had to make my eyes work extra hard. I really wanted to see the pictures. *It's the most beautiful book ever*, I thought. Of course, I ain't seen but a few books.

I look at it and look at it, turning the shiny pages real careful so I won't mess them up. I look at it every day after Hank leaves. Even in the dark I can see pretty ladies—pretty like Amy—wearing pretty clothes like I've never seen for real. Stella's clothes ain't nothing like these ladies' clothes. When she's not wearing her uniform, she wears the same pants every day with some different tops. When it's cold in the house she wears a sweater over her top.

My dress was pretty once. It had flowers that were bright pink and yellow but now are brown looking. I think it used to be Amy's. Amy taught me my colors. I remember that. I remember she taught me to count my numbers, too. Maybe it was Amy taught me to talk. My dress drags on the floor because it's too big. Sometimes a piece of it falls in the piss-pot. I try to hold it up so it won't fall in, but it hangs off me. I can't hold the whole thing up far enough. Sometimes when Hank comes to make sure I'm being good, he hollers at Stella that the bastard girl stinks and she should wash my dress. Then Stella pulls it over my head and leaves me naked for a day. Sometimes—especially when it's cold—I get real shivery waiting for my dress to come back from being washed. Leastwise it smells nice when I get it back. I try not to stink it up for a long time but sometimes Stella doesn't bring me any wiping paper. I wish I could reach that blanket covering the window. Sometimes I fall asleep thinking about how it would feel to wrap it around me—especially when Stella takes my dress for washing.

One day Stella wrapped me in her sweater so I wouldn't get cold waiting for my dress. Most days she gets home before Hank so she can have his dinner fixed and waiting. He gets real mad if his dinner ain't ready. Well, that day Hank got home first. He opened my door to see if I was being good. If I'd known it was him, I would've hid the sweater under my mattress and bunched up in the dark corner so he couldn't see me naked. When he saw me that way—wearing Stella's sweater—he got real mad and started hollering and hitting me.

When I was little, I figured out a trick to help me forget Hank's hitting and hollering. Whenever he'd light into me, I'd go someplace in my head—some place I heard about on the television box--like a beautiful garden with flowers in every color and grass that feels like soft carpet or one of those mattress commercials with fluffy blankets and pillows. I'd close my eyes real tight and stay there inside my head till Hank finished beating me. Whenever he got done, I'd come back to this room. Later when Stella would bring my water pan, I'd try to wash away the bad Hank-smell, but it didn't help much.

Anyway, when he found me wearing Stella's sweater, he pulled it up— and me with it—till I was lifted plum in the air and the buttons popped off. All the time, while he was shaking me out of that sweater, he was cussing and hollering. I dropped to the floor in a heap of bare skin trying to cover my naked body with my arms. Then he kicked my butt with his hard boot and I went flying. I curled into a ball and tried to make myself disappear. I knew what was coming next before he even lit into Stella. He caught her as soon as she walked in the door. I wish she wouldn't do stuff to make Hank mad cause I don't like to hear him beating her. It makes my belly feel sick. Besides, if he kills her, who'll bring me food?

Stella

Edith watches me like I'm gonna steal the silverware or something. She thinks I don't see her watchin' but I do. Oh, she's nice enough, but if she keeps askin' questions I'm gonna have to quit like I did my last job. Hank'll beat me if he don't get his drug and booze money. I'll have to find somethin' else real quick. I got to keep workin' so I can save enough money to get a lawyer for Amy and get me and Jodie outta that house.

Hank should be the one in prison, not Amy. It was *his* dope she got caught buyin.' It was because of Hank she got mixed up in the middle of a deal-gone-bad. She coulda' got killed. Instead she got caught and now she's rottin' in a prison cell. Hank won't let me go see her or write or call neither. He says she's the cause of all our troubles. I know what the cause of our troubles is, and it ain't Amy. It's Hank's drinkin' and druggin'. He can't hold a job for more than six months because he shows up to work drunk or high on dope or hung over. Sometimes we can't pay the rent on time, and sometimes I don't have enough grocery money to buy meat. We just eat noodles or rice that week.

I been savin' my tip money from the restaurant—hidin' it away under the kitchen sink. Hank don't look there since he don't do no cleanin' or cookin' or nothin'. I been puttin' it in a empty coffee can, and I got over two hundred dollars saved so far. I lied and told Hank that Edith don't allow us to take no tips. If he finds out I lied, he'll kill me.

Hank wasn't always mean as a snake, but his daddy was. Hank's daddy beat him and his brothers, too. I guess that's where he learnt it. When we first got married, he was a pretty good man--and hard workin'--but he always had a bad temper. I thought he was about the handsomest man I ever laid my eyes on with his thick blond curls and eyes as blue as a robin's egg. I was ready to leave my pappy--who never beat me but he never paid me much mind, neither. Mama loved me, I know, but she had to work all the time. I quit school when I was sixteen to go to work. Whenever I turned eighteen I run off and married Hank. We did okay for a while. He had a job at the paper mill, and I worked at the nursing home over in Hendersonville. We was savin' up to buy a house, but then I got pregnant and we didn't have no insurance. Even though Hank was stressed out by our money problems he was thrilled when we found out the baby was a boy. But it meant we had to put off buyin' that house.

I was nineteen when our baby boy was born and Hank was near thirty. We named him Henry after Hank and his daddy. I didn't 'specially like the name Henry for my sweet little boy but I supposed he'd grow into it one day. Henry was the purtiest little toe-headed boy you ever did see. He had Hank's blue eyes. As his hair grew, it sprung up with bouncy white curls all over his head. Henry adored his daddy, and Hank was proud as a peacock of that little boy. On the weekends, they stuck to each other like a magnet to a horseshoe.

Well, here's what happened. We was livin' in town in ol' Ms. Flannery's upstairs apartment. I still worked at the nursing home three days a week and helped Ms. Flannery with the cleanin', yard work, and such the other days. Whenever I worked at Hendersonville, she watched Henry for me.

It was the summer before my boy was fixin' to start kindygarten. He'd just turned five that August. The day was hot as all get-out. So, I opened every window I could, tryin' to get a breeze goin' through. Henry was playin' in his room with the new truck we got him for his birthday when Ms. Flannery called up the steps that she needed help carryin' the wash out to the clothesline. I told Henry to stay put and I'd be right back. I said I'd get him a grape

Popsicle from the icebox when I come back. Since grape was his favorite, I always ate the orange Popsicles and saved the grape for him.

Ms. Flannery and me was hangin' the clothes on the line when Henry come to the window. There was a window seat in his room. He liked to climb up and look at a book there or look out at the squirrels and rabbits in the backyard. I guess he heard our voices down there in the yard. So, he climbed up like usual. The next part I don't like to think about. It happened so fast. It was like one of them old Charlie Chaplin movies sped up to double time. But this weren't no movie. This was real, and it changed our lives forever.

Well, Henry leans forward to see me down there by the clothesline. He puts his hand on the window screen and out it pops just like that. Henry follows head-over-heels out that window and lands with a sickening thud on the ground two stories below. At first I froze. It was like all my muscles was paralyzed. It felt like a bad dream that I wanted to wake up from. Ms. Flannery drops a wet towel on the ground and starts runnin' but my feet won't move. In my gut, I know my baby's dead or hurt real bad. I don't want to know *how* bad. Next thing I remember, Ms. Flannery's screaming, "Oh, my God! Oh, my God!" Somehow my feet gets unstuck and next thing I'm cradling my broken boy in my arms, his head all floppy. Ms. Flannery must've called the ambulance because some paramedics or firemen or somebody showed up and tried to take my Henry from me. When I wouldn't let him go, they loaded us both on a stretcher and carried us to the ambulance. I don't remember any of this part but it's what Ms. Flannery told me later. I don't remember anything about the hospital neither till Hank showed up. That part I wish I could forget but it comes back in my dreams 'most every night: Hank rushin' into the E.R.; Hank seeing his dead son with the broken neck; Hank droppin' to the floor and hollerin' and cryin' till a nurse and two orderlies hold him down and give him a needle to make him quiet.

I held my dead baby all night and nobody tried to take him away. They wrapped him in a warm blanket and let me rock him and sing to him till the sun come up. Hank was passed out in the next bed. I didn't dare let myself start cryin' because I knew I wouldn't ever be able to stop. Somebody must've called my mama. She showed up the next day and she ended up stayin' near a month. She handled all the funeral arrangements, which I don't recall. She and Ms. Flannery done all the cookin' and cleanin' and washin'. They must've handled the visitors and the phone calls and whatever else needed handling 'cause it all got done, and I didn't do nothin' but lay in the bed. Hank took off after the funeral. When he come back a week or two later he weren't the same Hank and never has been since.

Chapter 2

Jodie

I wish Amy would come back from wherever she went. Sometimes she took me outside in the sunshine. There's a backyard outside this house. I remember it and I dream about it a lot. It has trees and a tall fence. Amy played with me there. She talked to me too. At night time, she sang songs to help me sleep, but I can't remember any. Oh, yes. I remember one. It went "Hush, little baby, don't cry…" or something like that, and there's a mocking bird in it. I still talk to Amy so I won't forget how to and so I can remember her face. I wait till Hank and Stella leave. Then I talk and talk—mostly in my head but sometimes whispering. I know Amy can't hear me but I make believe she can. I play games with her—the games she taught me like "I Spy with My Little Eye" and "Hop Scotch." The problem is there ain't much to spy in this room, and it's hard to hop with a strap on my ankle. Or is this my wrist? I get those two mixed up.

Sometimes I make believe Amy's sitting on my bed and we're looking at the picture book together. We talk about pretty clothes and going shopping to buy new dresses and shoes. I ain't ever been shopping at a store but I hear about it on the television box. There's a place called Target and one called

Walmart that gives you whatever you want. I wonder why Hank and Stella don't go there and get everything they talk about needing.

Hank says Stella don't make enough money and she spends too much on food. She says if he didn't buy drugs and booze, there'd be enough money for groceries. They yell and argue till Hank passes out or beats Stella to make her stop "bitchin'".

Sometimes I crawl on the hard floor and make believe I'm a dog named Sweetie, especially when Hank and Stella go out because I get tired of being with just me. Of course, I can't crawl far with this chain on my leg. I think Amy called me Sweetie or maybe I heard it on the television box.

First thing every morning, Hank turns on the television box and leaves it on all day. After he goes to work, Stella turns it to my favorite show, *Blue's Clues*. Blue is a dog who looks for clues to solve mysteries. I wish I could see the box because I want to see if Blue is a real blue dog. He must not be because I don't think real dogs are blue, and I don't think real dogs can talk like people. Sometimes at night I hear a dog barking outside and I wonder what it's saying. I wish I had a dog to talk to. It would sleep on my bed at night to keep me warm, and it would play with me when Hank and Stella ain't around. But if I had to share my food, that would be bad because Stella hardly brings enough for just me. I think she'd bring more if I asked but Hank would get mad. I know because sometimes when Hank gets sleepy-drunk in his chair and starts snoring, Stella quick throws me a piece of bread before he wakes up.

One time I got a whole chicken leg and I saved the bone. I guess Stella thought I ate it, bone-and-all but I saved it to make a doll. I had a doll once. Amy gave it to me. It had yellow yarn-hair and a checkered dress. I wonder what happened to that doll. Amy gave me a stuffed bear, too, but Hank threw it in the trash. My chicken-bone-doll ain't much of a doll but it's something to play with. I keep it way under my bed in the corner and play with it after Stella and Hank leave for work. I named it Amy and now I got somebody to talk to. I make believe that doll can talk to me. I make her say nice things like Amy used to, like... well, I can't remember exactly but I know she said nice things to me because I can still see her smiling. Sometimes I can feel her hugging me and rocking me back and forth. Sometimes I think I can even smell her hair.

Amy didn't like Hank. I remember that. She called him Daddy. He yelled at her and beat her—sometimes with his belt. I think Hank sent Amy away or maybe he killed her. I don't know. He tells Stella "Amy weren't nothin' but trouble. Got herself knocked up," he says. "Gave us another mouth to feed. Where's that good-for-nothin' baby-daddy now that the bastard girl's here? I don't see him bringin' home a paycheck to take care of his family."

"Maybe she needed a man to pay her some mind," Stella says quiet-like. Then louder she says, "Maybe she was lookin' for some love from a man since you never wanted her." Stella starts to get worked up. Sometimes she chances a beating because it's better than silence. "She knew you never wanted her. She knew you hated her!" Stella's screaming now and I know she's going to end up on the floor. Sure enough, Hank starts hitting her and calling her names. I sit in the darkest corner of my bed—my hands covering my ears—trying not to listen, but I can still hear.

The next day when Stella brings my food, she has black around one eye and her lip is all puffed up. It's Sunday and Hank is passed out drunk on the sofa. I can hear him snoring. Stella takes hold of my chin, looks in my eyes, and whispers, "It's gonna be all right, Baby. You'll see. One day it's gonna be all right." Why can't she just keep her mouth shut like I do? Why does she always have to start trouble? She knows how Hank is, but she says stuff that gets him riled.

Edith

Okay, that's it! I'm reporting that low-life creep! This morning, Stella showed up at work with a shiner and a lip the size of an orange. When I asked her about it she said she got up in the dark and fell down the stairs. Baloney! Why does she protect him? I'd have him hauled off to jail quicker than he could say jack rabbit.

Between shifts, I took Stella to my office in the back and tried to get her to come clean. I told her I knew she didn't fall down any stairs, and if she ever needed someone to talk to, I'd listen. By then I had cooled off some and I tried to speak gently, to win her trust. But she stuck to her story. That Hank has some hold on her. I don't want to make things worse for Stella, but I'm determined to find out what's going on. Mike will know what to do. I'll talk to Mike and see if he might be willing to snoop around a little on the q.t.

Sergeant Mike Travers—he's a cop that comes in every morning for breakfast, sometimes for dinner, too. Since his divorce last year, I think he gets lonely. From what I've heard about the former Mrs. Travers, Mike started feeling lonely long before that divorce. He's a good guy and not bad looking either, in my opinion. He keeps himself fit and well-groomed and he's easy to talk to. I could've told him Libby Marshall wasn't marriage material, but—like most of the men in this town—he was blinded by her beauty. He never would've listened to me. Personally, I don't think Libby was all that attractive. I'll admit she had a good figure with ample bosoms but her face was kind of hard—like someone who had "been around," if you know what I mean. Anyway, I'll talk to Mike the next time he shows up for dinner, after Stella has left for the evening. He owes me one or two favors from when he didn't have two nickels to rub together. That wife took him for what little he was worth and ran off with one of her man-friends. Mike got the house, but he had to sell it to pay off all the debts Libby piled up with her shopping addiction. I couldn't let him go hungry. So, I fed him at least one good meal a day and sometimes two. "Edith," he'd say, "You're one of the good ones. I don't know how I would've survived without your kindness."

"Hey, you're doing *me* a favor," I'd say, trying to spare him embarrassment. "You should see all the leftover food I throw out every day. I'd rather have you eat it than throw it in the dumpster."

Chapter 3

Jodie

Somebody came to the door this morning. I knew it was morning because Hank and Stella just left for work and *Curious George* was on the television box. I was starting to play with my Amy-Doll when the doorbell rang. It rang maybe three times. Then the knocking starts and I hear, "Police! Is anybody home? Open up!" More knocking and shouting. Then some talking on the porch. I stay real quiet—like Hank says I better if I don't want a beating. I hold my breath for a long time, trying not to make a sound. Finally, they give up and leave.

Mike

We've had complaints before about that shack on the edge of town. It's hard to believe anybody lives there in such a squalid condition but that's the address Edith gave me. The neighbors complain the yard's a mess—which it is—and the roof is starting to cave in. We've gotten reports of yelling and suspected domestic disputes. We've sent beat cops to check it out more than once but every time, a woman—must be Stella—comes to the door and says everything's fine. There's not much we can do unless she's willing to press charges. Some states, like Virginia, have mandatory arrest laws. If an officer simply suspects domestic violence has occurred, he must arrest the suspect. Unfortunately for Stella, this law doesn't apply in North Carolina.

I'm going to do some research and see what I can find out about the situation. I owe it to Edith. I don't know what I would've done if she hadn't kept me fed last year after Libby plunged me into debt and ran off with that no-good Ralph. Well, good riddance to both of them, I say. Within the first year of marrying Libby, I knew I had made a mistake. I guess love really is blind. Truthfully, it was more lust than love. I felt proud to have a sexy woman take an interest in me, especially when she could have had any man in this town. In retrospect, she probably *did* have most of them. Anyway, Edith has a good head on her shoulders. If she thinks Stella is being abused by her husband, you can bet there's something to it.

A couple of years ago, before I made sergeant, we had a training session with a speaker from the Domestic Violence Center. Everybody working at the station was required to attend. We learned that battered women are usually brainwashed by the batterer to think they deserve to be beaten. That's why they stay with their abusers. They think they're to blame. It's called Battered Woman Syndrome. It doesn't seem logical, but it certainly explains why a victim will deny she is being beaten. She feels shame and guilt. Anyway, I'm going to ask the captain if he'll assign a detective to see what can be dug up on ol' Hank Leonard. Maybe I'll just do a little snooping around, myself, too.

Chapter 4

Jodie

I couldn't sleep last night. Besides being cold, my leg hurt where the chain is strapped on. Sometimes it rubs till I get a sore there. This was more than a sore. I wanted to cry, but I knew Hank would hear me and give me a beating. So, I lay there on the bare mattress, my leg throbbing and me trying not to moan till Stella came with my food. She saw my leg swelled up and lopping over the strap, and she hollered for Hank. "I don't care what you do to me," she shouted, "but this baby don't deserve to be treated worse than a gutter dog!"

"She ain't nothin' but a bastard!" Hank says, pushing the door so hard it hits the wall with a bang. "What's goin' on in here, anyhow? I got to get to work and you wastin' my time with the bastard girl!" I can tell he's hung over like usual. His eyes are all red and he's moving real slow, like his arms and legs are heavy. I wish Stella hadn't seen my leg. Now we're both going get beat. I want to say, "Stop, Stella! Don't say any more." But she's getting all worked up and starting to holler like Hank.

"Take that damn chain offa her leg!" screams Stella. "Can't you see it's infected?" He up and slaps her with the back of his hand, and she falls on the floor hard, her cane flying out of her hand.

"Who the hell you think yer talkin' to, woman?"

I've never seen Stella fight back before, not lately anyhow. Mostly she tries to keep quiet and keep Hank from getting madder. But she gets up—even without her cane—and pushes Hank and starts beating on his chest, arms flailing, and hitting him like she's a wild animal. She's crying and hollering, "She's yer granddaughter, for God's sake!" That did it. Hank hauls off and punches her hard in the belly. This time she stays down, holding her belly and groaning. Then he comes for me. I knew it was coming. He jerks on the chain so hard I think my leg'll fall off. It hurts something awful and I can't help but holler.

"Nothin' but trouble just like yer mama!" he screams. The next part I don't remember because I passed out, I guess. When I come to the chain is on my other leg, there's a ice pack on my hurting leg, and I'm covered with a blanket—a soft, warm blanket. I'm pretty sure it's still daytime when I hear Stella in the kitchen. She must have stayed home from work. Leastwise, I hope it's Stella.

Edith

Stella called in sick this morning. She sounded terrible. I asked her if I could do anything for her and she said "no," that she just needed to rest and she'd be in tomorrow for sure. "Stomach trouble," she said. I didn't buy it for a second. I anticipated she'd come in the next day with fresh bruises she couldn't explain. How many times can one person fall down the stairs, anyway?

Mike promised to check into the situation. He said we must be careful not to make matters worse for Stella. Of course, I understand how important it is to proceed slowly. I've read about similar situations where the cops moved in without sufficient evidence, and the abuser got off Scott-free only to come back and murder the victim. I just feel so bad for Stella. I'd like to strangle that good-for-nothing husband of hers.

Stella

I really messed up this time, but when I seen Jodie's leg all swolled and red, I just lost it. I don't know what took me over. I couldn't stop myself from lightin' into Hank. All the beatin', all the meanness and ugly names didn't matter. It wasn't about me. It was about that pitiful, helpless child. Even in the dark I could see her little face contorted in agony, but she didn't make a sound—not till Hank jerked on the chain. It made me sick to see how much it hurt her. All she ever did to make Hank hate her was to get born, and that weren't even her choice.

He punched me harder than he ever has before, and I thought I'd never be able to get up. But I made myself stay conscious for Jodie. No tellin' what he woulda' done to her if I hadn't kept my wits about me. I whispered, "Help me, Jesus," and suddenly I couldn't feel nothin' hurting. I said (real sweet-like), "Hank Honey, now you better let me take care of that leg or else you'll end up at the E. R. with a lot of explaining to do." He dropped Jodie's leg hard on the mattress and turned like he was gonna' light into me again. That's when the poor baby girl screamed and passed out cold from the pain. I was still layin' on the floor when I spoke again, my words drippin' with honey. "We don't want no cops comin' around askin' questions now, do we, Hank? You better let me take care of that leg so it don't get no worse."

Hank stomps outta the room, cussin' like a sailor. I don't dare move. At least Jodie ain't feelin' no pain, so I stay put. I feel like I'm gonna upchuck but I swallow hard till the urge passes. I think my nose is broke. It's bleedin' down my uniform and throbs like all get-out. I'm thinkin', *By the time I get cleaned up, I'm gonna miss the bus. What if Edith fires me? What if she calls the cops? She ain't gonna swallow that story about me fallin' down the stairs again. We ain't even got no stairs but she don't know it.*

Hank stomps back with a padlock key and unfastens the strap from Jodie's leg. I'm prayin' he leaves it off, but no. He just switches it to her other leg. "See to that ankle," he says, "and you best work a miracle 'cause if it gets worse, it'll be you takin' her to the hospital and you explainin' how it happened—just like you explainin' how my boy fell outta the window on your watch, bitch!"

When I heard the front door slam, I shoulda' felt relieved, but I just felt lower than a snake. Hank was right. It *was* my fault our precious boy fell to his death. I shouldn't have left him alone. I should've noticed the screen was loose. It was my fault Hank started drinkin' and worse. It's my fault Amy's in prison and it'll be my fault if this baby girl dies.

I crawled on my hands and knees to the kitchen and grabbed onto the counter to pull myself up. I washed the blood off my face and neck and pulled a bag of frozen peas outta the freezer. *Maybe I can keep my nose from gettin' too swolled up.* I felt like my ribs was broke from where Hank punched me. My side hurt every time I moved or breathed but I had to take care of Jodie's leg. Since there was only one bag of frozen vegetables I poured ice cubes into a plastic bag and crushed 'em with a rolling pin. Now I had to figure how to get back to Jodie's room without my cane and carryin' two ice packs, but first I had to call Edith.

I wish Edith wouldn't be so nice to me. It makes me feel worse for lyin' to her. I wish she'd stop askin' so many questions, too—just let me do my job and pick up my paycheck. Anyways, she let me have the day off. Now I can nurse Jodie and maybe have me some peace for a few hours.

Chapter 5

Jodie

Stella stayed in my room most all day. She's never done that before. I could tell she was hurting as much as me but she wrapped me in a blanket. She held me and rocked me like Amy used to. With that blanket around me I felt warm and safe for the first time since I don't know when. I knew it would only last till Hank came home. Stella gave me some pills—to ease the hurt in my leg—and fed me soup. She kept changing the ice packs, too, mine and hers. She talked to me the most she ever has and she cried a lot. "Honey," she said, "I'm so sorry for this mess we got ourselves in. I thought Hank would get better someday but he just gets worse. It's them drugs. We got to get outta here and go where Hank can't find us. We got to get Amy—your mama—outta prison, too." When I heard Stella call Amy my mama I said the first word anybody heard me say out loud in a long, long time.

"Mama?" I asked, looking up at Stella's face. Stella—her eyes used to the dark now—looked at me like she seen a ghost. Then she hugged me and started crying and rocking again.

She said, "Yes, Jodie, Amy is your mama and she loves you. I love you, too, but Hank won't let me take proper care of you. I'm so sorry, Jodie! It ain't right for you to be chained up in this here dark room all alone. It ain't right for you to suffer for my sins."

As much as my leg was hurting, my heart was jumping for joy because now I knew Amy was my mama and now I knew I had a name, a real name: Jodie. My name is Jodie.

After that day, Stella seemed different. As broken down as we both were Stella seemed like she got stronger—more stubborn-like. It seemed like she wasn't afraid of Hank anymore, at least not so much. Whenever she came to see me, she'd whisper something like, "Don't you fret, Jodie. I'm gonna get us outta here." Whenever Hank passed out drunk—sometimes even in the night—she'd bring me extra food. She didn't even seem afraid of getting caught. I don't know where her nerve came from but she seemed daring-like. She'd say, "You gotta be strong when we make our break." It scared me how brave she got because I knew if she stood up to Hank again she'd get beat worse than ever. He might even kill her. Then, what would happen to me and Amy, my mama?

It took a few days, but my leg got better. Stella made me soak it in a bucket of warm salt water morning and night and ice it in between whenever she came home from work. She talked Hank into letting her wrap a dish towel around my good leg so it wouldn't rub against the strap and get infected, too. At night, I'd take that towel and cover me up. It felt so nice to be covered at night, even by a thin towel. Sometimes I fell into a deep sleep for a change.

Once my leg got better, Hank wouldn't let Stella come as much. I missed her taking care of me (especially her holding and rocking me), and I missed that bucket of warm water. I missed the soft blanket. But mostly I missed Amy. Now I knew Amy was my mama and she was alive. I started dreaming about us being together again for real. But how? How could Stella get us out of this place and away from Hank?

Mike

I did some digging into Hank Leonard's background and made some very interesting discoveries. I found a whole series of newspaper articles about his daughter, Amy Leonard, from three years ago. The articles said she was accused and convicted of being a drug dealer—cocaine and other narcotics. I recall reading about that trial now. I remember thinking the young woman in the pictures didn't look like a junkie or a dealer, either, for that matter. Even in her mug shot, she looked more like the all-American girl next door— young, blonde, and pretty with striking blue, sad eyes. She was sentenced to six years in the state correctional facility for women. So, she'd be about halfway through her stint by now. What could make a smart, pretty, young woman—with her whole life ahead of her—throw away her future by getting involved in the drug scene?

I used to think our quiet, little town couldn't possibly have a drug problem, maybe a little weed at the high school, but coke and heroin? That's some serious stuff. Then I entered the police force and got a reality check. I plan to do some more investigating on my own before trying to question Stella. According to Edith, she's very tight-lipped about her home life. I feel sure she wouldn't open up to a man, especially one in law enforcement. Maybe Edith can win her trust eventually. If Edith's instincts about abuse are true, Stella might be more likely to talk to another woman than a man.

Edith

The morning after Stella called in sick, she reported for the breakfast shift right on time. Her nose was swollen at the bridge and she had two shiners that she had tried to cover with yellow-tinted concealer. It took every ounce of my self-control not to react to Stella's appearance, but I had to be careful not to alienate her. Mike had advised me to move cautiously. I sensed this woman was living in mortal danger. As much as I wanted to help, I had read enough about battered women to know that proceeding too quickly could increase her risk. Somehow, I needed to keep Stella out of the public's view for a few days, at least until her bruises faded. If her customers made comments—which they surely would—Stella might spook. Who knows? She might even quit her job. I could lose contact with her and then how could I possibly be of any help? No. I needed to act as cool as possible, giving Mike time to investigate and gather concrete evidence against Hank (that creep)— evidence to put him away for a long time. *Okay Edith, here she comes. Think fast.*

"Good morning, Stella. Welcome back," I said as nonchalantly as possible. As usual, Stella stored her ragged purse in the kitchen broom closet. "Feeling better today?" I asked, taking care not to glance up from my vegetable chopping.

"Doin' fine," Stella responded diffidently, avoiding direct eye-contact. "Sorry about yesterday. I'll just get to settin' the tables."

"Um, actually, I need you in the kitchen today. I, um… the pantry needs to be inventoried. I already got Melinda to cover your tables just in case you were still sick today."

"I never done that inventory thing before," said Stella.

"Oh, don't worry. I'll get you started. You'll be fine."

"Okay, then, if you show me what to do," she said. As I led her to the storage room, I was relieved that Stella appeared not to suspect my motive. I admit to feeling a little pride at my own quick thinking, too. Now I just needed to keep her busy in the rear of the restaurant—away from the customers and wait staff without arousing her suspicion.

Later, when I checked her progress, I noticed Stella had dragged a chair into the storage room. I couldn't remember the last time I saw her sit on the job. She winced, holding her right side whenever she thought I wasn't looking. How I wished I could help her! At least I could offer a listening ear, if only she'd let me. But, of course, she must think she can't trust anyone. According to Mike, telling the truth could actually make things worse for her. At least while she's at work, she's away from that horrid monster. What would I do if he ever showed up here? I don't know. Her working here could endanger all of our lives. Yikes! I just thought of that.

Stella

Edith put me to work in the back today, doing inventory. I guess I felt relieved with my side hurtin' and all. Carrying them heavy trays would've been extra hard, for sure. But I wouldn't earn no tips workin' in the storage room. I counted on them tips. I figured once I had about a thousand dollars saved I could afford to leave Hank and take me and Jodie somewhere safe. Then I'd get another job and save up to hire a lawyer for Amy.

Whenever Hank first put Jodie in that room and strapped her leg to the bed, I begged and begged him not to. I begged him to let her loose. *Where could someone even buy a strap and chain like that?* I wondered. I pleaded with him to let me give her a blanket. She didn't do nothin' wrong. "She should be goin' to school," I said. "She should be playin' outside in the sunshine like other kids."

"Kids like Henry, you mean? Like my Henry who's dead because of you?" he'd shout. Every time I brought it up, he'd remind me about Henry. Then, he'd hit me and call both of us awful names. Finally, I had to let it go. I was afraid he'd kill her and me both.

Edith says I got a good head for figures. It feels nice that she trusts me to do inventory but I sure need that extra money. A couple times I thought about takin' a little bit outta the register every day but, as careful as Edith is with money, she'd notice. I can't afford to lose this job, neither, and I can't be gettin' myself arrested. Then who'd take care of Jodie? Besides, I like Edith.

She's a good woman and a fair boss.

More'n once, I thought about killin' Hank in his sleep. I could make it look like somebody broke in and robbed the place or maybe I could make it look like a drug overdose. Every time it comes down to not havin' enough money to run away and start over. No. I gotta be patient. I gotta work hard and wait till the time is right. What makes me impatient is watching my poor, innocent grandbaby suffering. I feel so helpless and alone. I used to feel sorry for Hank but not no more. I don't exactly hate him because I know it's my fault he turned out this way. Sometimes I feel like I deserve to get beat up. Sometimes I feel like killing myself, but then I remember Jodie and how I can't bear the thought of failing her like I failed my Henry and my Amy. I just can't leave this world knowin' I failed everybody I ever loved—even Hank who I once loved.

Chapter 6

Edith

I kept Stella busy in the storage room for a couple of days. Her bruises began to fade from purple to yellow but were still visible. Her nose started to shrink to its normal size, but she still held her side whenever she thought no one was looking. I could tell she was in pain. The third day, I asked her to inventory the contents of the walk-in freezer and record the new shipment of dry goods. By Thursday, I had run out of jobs. Her regular customers were asking about her, and I started feeling guilty for telling them she was on vacation. Not only was I trying to spare her from answering their inevitable questions, but I could tell her regular waitressing duties would be painful for her.

When Mike came for dinner Thursday evening, he took his usual seat at the counter. I brought him the blue plate special—which happened to be roast beef, mashed potatoes, and peas—and, as usual, we chatted about this-and-that while he ate and I checked out customers at the cash register. Mike is a good listener. He and I just feel at ease with each other. Lately our conversations invariably include Stella.

"Did you know Stella and Hank had a son?" Mike asked.

"No kidding! She never talks about any children. She doesn't talk much at all, especially about her personal life. Where is her son now?"

"He's dead," Mike said, between mouthfuls of mashed potato dripping with gravy. "Died when he was barely five years old."

"Oh, Mike! That poor woman. What happened?"

"According to the police report, he fell from a third story window and died on impact."

"Merciful heavens! That good-for-nothing husband of hers. It was him, wasn't it?"

"No, no. He wasn't even home at the time. It was ruled an accident. Stella and Hank were renting an apartment in the old Flannery house at the time. You know… that three-story place down on Crescent Avenue. Somebody bought it a couple years ago and fixed it up really nice."

"No wonder she doesn't talk about her life. So much pain," I said, as I tried to erase the mental image of a five-year-old hurtling to his death. "How long ago did it happen?"

"The boy would be a grown man now if he had lived. As I recall, the report was from 1989. Less than a year later Stella gave birth to a girl."

"Really? Where is she now? Did you find out anything about her?"

"Her name is Amy, and she's doing time over at Women's Correctional for possession of drugs."

I couldn't believe what I was hearing. Stella had worked for me almost two years and had never said one word about her children, or Hank, for that matter. Under the circumstances, I could understand why she'd be embarrassed to discuss her personal life but I felt guilty—like I should know her better by now. She needed a friend—that was clear—but she must have felt she couldn't trust anyone not to judge her or betray her awful secrets.

"What can I do to help? How can I get her to open up to me?"

"I think you have to respect her privacy, Edith, at least for now."

"But her life must be a living-hell," I said, "and she has no one to turn to for support as far as I can tell."

"She must be stronger than she looks or she wouldn't have survived this long."

"You're right, of course, but I do have one idea."

"What's that?" asked Mike.

"I've been reading about Battered Woman Syndrome on the Internet. It says one of the main reasons women stay with their abusers is financial. They usually don't have the means to make it on their own. Actually, Stella is lucky Hank allows her to work. From what I've read, typically the abuser tries to isolate the woman from all outside contacts."

"Yeah, that's the usual pattern, but I think Hank needs Stella's money to help him maintain his drug habit."

"Hank is a junkie? That explains a lot. Can you charge him for using and get him sent away?"

"Hopefully, but we have to be careful. We must have ironclad evidence or he'll get off on a technicality. Then his violence could escalate and really put Stella's life in danger."

"Have you seen her face this week? I think she's lucky to be alive."

"Listen, Edith, I know you're worried about her, but give me some time to gather more information, okay? I promise I'm working on it, but I must proceed cautiously. I'm not actually a detective, you know."

"Okay, Mike. I trust you. Keep me posted, will you?"

"You bet. Hey. Tell that cranky chef of yours the roast beef was dry."

"Was it? Oh, dear."

"No. It was delicious, but we don't want Louie getting a bigger head than he already has, do we?"

"Shove off, troublemaker."

Mike grabbed his cap and jacket from the hook where he always hung them and headed for the door, then turned back to face me. "Wait. You didn't tell me about your idea."

"Tomorrow," I said, waving his twenty-dollar bill in the air. As Mike exited the café it occurred to me that I looked forward to his daily visits and would miss our conversations if he decided to take his meals elsewhere. I had never thought about it much before but had to admit I was attracted to the man, especially in his uniform. Of course, no one could ever replace my sweet, Charlie, who died too young, but Mike surely had become a good friend.

Stella

Edith called me to her office this morning. I was afraid she was gonna say I did something wrong on the inventory. I was real surprised when she said what a good job I was doin', especially after me callin' in sick on Monday. She said, "Stella, you're a good worker and smart, too. I noticed what a thorough job you did on the inventory. All your figures came out right. I've been thinking I'd like to take some time off to visit my family and maybe get some projects done at home."

"Yes, Ma'am," I said so she'd know I was listenin'.

"I was wondering if you'd be willing to become my assistant manager. You know, take over when I'm not here." Before I could answer she added,

"I know you wouldn't be able to cover the dinner shift but that shouldn't be a problem."

"You mean I wouldn't be waitin' tables no more?"

"That's right. You'd be in charge of the wait staff and Louie and the busboys, too. And you'd get a significant raise."

"More money?" I asked, not because I hadn't heard her, but because it sounded too good to be true.

"Yes. What do you think?"

I didn't know what to say. I was stunned that Edith would trust me with that much responsibility. I wasn't sure I could handle it. Also, I felt ashamed of myself for thinkin' about stealin' from the till before. But more money would get me closer to being able to leave Hank and getting Jodie outta that awful place. I was just about to accept her offer when something popped into my head.

"Um, meanin' no disrespect, Ms. Edith… I mean I feel real honored you thinkin' I could do the job, but, um…" I was embarrassed to bring up the subject, but I had to.

"What is it, Stella?" she asked.

"Well, it's just that… I wouldn't be gettin' no more tips, would I?"

"No, but I can assure you the extra pay will more than compensate for your tip money."

I should've been thrilled with her answer. I could tell she was expectin' me to be thrilled, but what was goin' through my head was Hank seein' my paychecks. He made me sign 'em and hand 'em over every Friday as soon as he walked through the door. Hank would take that extra money and put it straight into drugs and beer. Then, where would Jodie and me be?

"Do you want some time to think about it, Stella?" she asked. I could tell by her tone she was disappointed in my answer.

"No, Ma'am," I said. "I appreciate your offer and I'll work real hard. I promise."

"I have no doubt about that, Stella, and please call me Edith, especially now that you're an assistant manager," she said, smiling.

"Okay, Edith," I said, trying to sound natural, but I know I giggled uncomfortable-like. "Um, Ma'am, Edith, can I ask a favor?"

"Of course."

"Well, I was wonderin'. That extra pay… would it be possible for me to get it in cash?"

For a second or two Edith looked stunned, and I thought for sure she was gonna' take back her offer, but then she looked straight at me like she understood what I was askin'. Of course, she couldn't know why I was askin'.

I ain't never told her nothin' about Hank. So how could she know? Then, slowly nodding, she said, "Let me see what I can do. We'll start your training first thing Monday morning."

"Yes, Ma'am. Thank you, Ma'am." Now I let my excitement show. I couldn't help it. No one ever put faith in me before like Edith did. She was givin' me a chance to make somethin' of myself. I was so beholden. I sure wanted to do a good job and make her proud. I didn't want to disappoint her, but I knew as soon as I had enough money saved up, me and Jodie (and Amy, too) would have to move far, far away from this here town.

Jodie

Tonight, when Stella came to bring my food she looked different. Happier, somehow. She came close and gave me a hug. I knew Hank must be passed out or she wouldn't take the chance of talking to me. She sat on my bed real careful so the springs wouldn't squeak and she put me on her lap. Then she whispered to me, all the time watching the door.

"Sweetie," she said, "I'm gettin' us outta here real soon."

Her holding me felt so good. I wanted to stay on her lap forever with her arms around me like that. I wanted to believe what she was saying, but I was scared to. I knew Hank would never let me out, and if Stella tried to get me out, he'd kill us both.

"Baby," she said real quiet, "I promise one day soon you and me and your mama are gonna be free. I got a plan now and everything's gonna be okay. Now, eat your rice and beans and don't give Hank no trouble this weekend." She set me on the bed with my bowl and spoon and left the room.

How can I give anybody trouble strapped to the bed like I am day and night? Sometimes I just want to jerk and jerk this here chain till it pulls the bed apart. I want to scream real loud and run, run, run... if I can remember how to run. But where will I go? Who'll feed me? How can I ever find Amy—I mean Mama? Besides, if I run away, Hank'll kill Stella for sure. Mostly I try not to think about stuff because it makes me sad, but tonight I can't help it because of what Stella told me. Tonight, I need to cry a lot but first I got to eat.

I want to talk to Stella, especially since she talks to me now, but I'm scared to. She keeps saying she has a plan. I want to ask her about it. I want to ask her about Amy. If Hank catches me talking he'll light into us both and maybe stop Stella coming in my room. No. I can't chance it.

Mike

At every opportunity, I do more snooping—I prefer to call it research—about the Leonards, partly because I owe it to Edith and partly because I'm just as concerned as she is about Stella's situation. I wonder if Stella knows about the Agape Shelter for Women and Children. If Hank is abusing her, she could get away from him and stay there for a while. Since the location is undisclosed, he wouldn't be able to find her. Agape also provides services to help women get back on their feet, both financially and emotionally. We keep a supply of information brochures at the station. Maybe I could place some discreetly in Edith's café. Yeah, that's what I'll do. Tomorrow when I stop in for dinner, I'll give Edith some of those pamphlets to put where Stella can't help but see them.

Yesterday I asked Ted, one of the detectives, to look into Amy's trial. I tried to clear it with the captain first but he insisted the case couldn't be reopened. "Amy Leonard was caught red-handed in possession of narcotics and that's that," he said.

Something about her indictment smells fishy to me, though. First, I discovered Amy was an honor roll student at St. Stephens High but she never graduated. Unofficially, I talked to past-principal Andy Martin—who happens to be one of Edith's regular customers. Andy's retired now but he remembered Amy because of the publicity surrounding her trial. He said Amy was smart and quiet and stayed out of trouble. She even made the National Honor Society. Then, suddenly she dropped out of school in the middle of her senior year. According to Andy some kind of "family situation" caused her to quit school—like her father was dying or something. A year later she was working at Winn Dixie and earning her GED. Andy suggested we talk to the guidance counselor, Ms. Rutherford, who still works at the school. I figure if I can come up with some concrete evidence showing there were questionable circumstances surrounding Amy's arrest, maybe I can convince Captain Howard to look into it. It's not like the detectives in this tiny precinct are overloaded with cases.

Chapter 7

Jodie

One morning I wake up real early, at least I think it's early because I don't hear Hank or Stella moving around and I don't smell coffee like usual. There's birds chirping outside my window. Spring must be coming. I wish I could go outside and see the birds. I lay awake real still, feeling cold. I move to the end of the bed—where my leg is strapped—so I can tuck both legs inside my dress, but I'm still shivery. Thinking about birds helps me forget how cold I feel. I remember what they look like and how quick-like they move to peck at stuff on the ground. Birds can fly in the air too. Sometimes I dream I can fly. Then, I don't want to wake up because it feels so free up in the sky. If I had wings like birds, I could fly way up high where Hank can't reach me. Then, I could fly far away from here. I wonder what birds eat. Maybe I can eat what birds eat, so nobody needs to bring me food.

Spring is when flowers pop up out of the ground. I remember Amy made flowers grow in the dirt by the back stoop. They were pretty colors like yellow and purple. She said flowers was God's handiwork. I don't know what that means. I just remember her saying it. She showed me how to water the flowers with a sprinkler can. Lately, I been remembering more stuff about

Amy. I like thinking about her, but remembering makes me cry, too. I miss Amy—my mama. I wish she would come and take me out of here. Then, maybe I can see flowers again and birds, too.

After a bit, I hear somebody stirring in the kitchen. I hope it's Stella. I don't ever hope it's Hank. It must be Stella because Hank always turns on the television box first thing. This is the day when Hank goes out to get more drugs, I think. Stella stays here to clean and cook and wash clothes. After Hank leaves, she brings me extra food. Then she washes me and cleans my teeth. If Hank knew she done all that he'd beat her something awful. Then he'd beat me.

Stella takes my dress for washing and wraps me in a towel. Being warm feels so good. I know it'll get her in trouble if Hank comes home too soon. Stella says, "Now you wrap up in this towel, Baby, but if you hear the front door open, hide it under the mattress real quick. I'll bring your dress as soon as it's dry."

I want to stay wrapped up in this here towel. It feels so warm. I must have fell asleep waiting for my dress because I didn't hear Hank coming through the squeaky front door. Before I know it, he's pushing the door to my room hard. Like usual, it bangs the wall and wakes me up. I can tell Hank's drugged up with dope, and I know trouble's coming for sure. Stella hobbles in after Hank and sees me trying to hide the towel and hide me, too. I curl up in the corner as far as the strap'll let me. Hank gets to me and grabs the towel. He starts slapping at my bare skin and punching my back. I know Stella's going to be next. I bet she knows it, too, but she climbs on the bed and pulls at Hank trying to get him off me. I get real scared now because I think he'll kill her for sure. She's saying things like, "Come on, Hank. Don't bother yourself with her. I'll fix you some nice fresh coffee. Let's see if there's any of them donuts left." She's trying to act all calm but I can tell she's scared like me. Anyway, I know it won't work because when Hank gets high he can't hear nothing. He just acts all crazy—hollering, throwing stuff, and beating on her and me. I try to cover wherever I think he'll hit me, but I ain't got but two hands. My back stings where Hank slapped it, and my head's hurting where he punched it and pulled my hair.

Hank stands up and throws Stella off his back. She catches herself with her cane and leans against the wall to keep from falling. He tries to punch her but he can't walk straight. He misses and almost lands on the floor. She's walking backwards out of the room now and he's following her all the time punching the air and cussing about the "bastard girl" and the "worthless bitch." I think Stella knows if she can get Hank to a chair, he'll pass out and sleep till suppertime, like usual.

In the next room, I hear more hollering and hitting. I hear Stella begging Hank to stop and him calling her names. I hear her cane drop to the floor, then something breaking, and Stella trying to get Hank to calm down. Then it gets quiet out there, and I hope Hank is asleep. When Stella comes back, I'm shaking and shivering, partly because Hank flung the towel across the room, and partly because I'm hurting, but mostly because I been afraid he killed Stella.

Finally, Stella wraps the towel around me again and brings me some milk. She sits on the bed—holding me real soft-like—and cries and cries. "I'm so sorry, Jodie Honey. I'm so sorry," she keeps whispering over and over. "He won't hurt us no more today." That means Hank is passed out and it's safe for me to cry, too.

Stella has blood coming out of her mouth, but she's mostly okay. I know she saved me from getting beat worse. I don't feel like drinking the milk, but I know I might not get any tomorrow. So, I drink it down.

Mike

We got another call about a suspected domestic dispute at Stella's address. It came in to the station at thirteen-ten Saturday. By the time Joe and Greg arrived on the scene all was quiet. In fact, ol' Hank was sprawled on the sofa sawing logs. He didn't even wake up when they pounded on the door. Stella answered the door. As usual, she told the officers everything was fine. She claimed to have dropped some pots and pans trying to get them out of the cupboard and said one hit her in the mouth, causing her to scream. Greg said he wasn't sure, but it looked like she had lost a tooth.

Next, the guys went across the street to talk to the neighbor who had called in the complaint. The woman told them she had been working in her garden earlier when she heard sounds of a scuffle with a lot of yelling and what sounded like objects breaking. She also reported she had seen Hank come home just before that, looking like he was drunk in the middle of the day.

"Had he been driving?" Joe asked.

"Yes, he pulled up in that heap," she said, pointing to Hank's old beat up Chevy truck.

"Would you be willing to testify to that in a court of law?" asked Greg. At this point, the woman—who had been quite animated in describing the earlier events—began to back down.

"Listen, officers," she said nervously. "I have to live in this neighborhood. If that woman is getting beaten by her no-good husband, he should be stopped, but I can't get involved. I have children. With his violent temper, what's to stop him from coming after us or our children?"

"How well do you know Mrs. Leonard? Do you two talk?" Joe wanted to know.

"No, we're not friendly at all. She takes the bus to work every day during the week, and on the weekends her husband is home... except for Saturday mornings that is."

The guys asked her to keep an eye on the house and call right away if she witnessed anything else of a suspicious nature. Joe said he didn't expect to hear from her again.

Edith will know if Stella comes to work Monday with a tooth missing. I need to gather some concrete evidence against Hank before he kills her. But how? If she won't admit to being beaten and won't press charges...

I'm convinced their daughter, Amy, holds the key to shedding light on this situation and maybe putting Hank away, but if Captain Howard won't let me or any of the detectives investigate, where does that leave me? Worse yet, where does that leave Stella?

The captain didn't say I couldn't go to the prison for a friendly visit, unofficially, of course. Maybe I can get Edith to go with me. Amy might be more likely to talk to a woman than a male cop, anyway.

Stella

Hank is gettin' more violent by the day. I think he woulda killed Jodie yesterday if I hadn't got him outta that room. He don't need a reason. Just needs to get high on them drugs and he turns into a human wrecking ball, destroying everything and everyone in his way. I managed to get him outta her room, but then he punched me so hard in the mouth he knocked out a tooth. The only good part about them drugs is the more dope he takes the longer he sleeps. When that wears off he starts drinkin'. He'll polish off a six-pack before bedtime and another one Sunday. It's the same every weekend. Only God knows how he manages to get up Monday mornings and go to work. Of course, he's hung over but he takes some of them uppers to keep him going during the week. If I didn't make enough wages to pay the rent, we'd be out on the street. I can't let him find out I'll be making more money soon. He'll just spend it on his habit, and us barely having enough to eat as it is.

Before the cops showed up, I managed to get myself cleaned up pretty good and the mess on the floor, too. Hank was passed out on the sofa. That woman across the way musta called 'em. She works in her yard a lot and probably heard us yelling and Hank breaking stuff. I wish folks would just mind their own business. I don't want nobody knowing how Hank treats me. They'll think I'm nothin' but trash… and if they knowed about Jodie… I ain't sure what would happen. I'm thinking the cops would turn us in to Child Protective Services and I'd never see her again.

I gotta get Jodie and me outta here, and soon. I've looked and looked for that key—the one that unlocks the strap around Jodie's ankle—but Hank has it hid real good. Whenever he goes out for his booze and dope, I look. I even get up in the middle of the night sometimes and search through Hank's stuff. When we get ready to run, I decided, I'll take a sharp knife or some other tool and cut through the leather strap to free Jodie. I wonder if she remembers how to walk. She don't weigh no more than a kitten. I can carry her if I need to. The problem is I don't know if I can carry her all the way to the bus station. I gotta have a plan. I gotta have everything in place so nothin' goes wrong. Social Services can't never know about Jodie. We gotta go where Hank can't never find us.

Edith

Mike thinks we should visit the Women's Correctional Facility in Hendersonville and have a talk with Stella's daughter, Amy. It sounds like a good idea to me. Somehow, we have to dig up fresh information to convince Mike's captain to reopen her case. Mainly we hope she can tell us about the relationship between Hank and Stella. I sense that—more than ever—Stella's life is in danger, and I want to know if Mike can pin something on Hank that will get him put away for a long time.

I think I'll pick up a few toiletries to take to Amy. I don't know if she'll be allowed to keep them but, if I were locked up in a place like that, I'd want to have some nice soaps and lotions—something to make me feel feminine.

In the meantime, I'll be training Stella for her new position. At first, she was hesitant to accept my offer. She didn't think she could handle the added responsibility. She has such low self-esteem. I can tell she's intelligent but she doesn't feel the least bit confident. She did a great job on the inventory and she never makes a mistake on the customer's bills. That husband of hers has beaten every ounce of self-worth out of her, I'd say. I almost blew it when she asked for her raise in cash. It took me a minute to realize why. She needs to keep Hank in the dark about the extra money so he won't take it. I wish I could pay her more but my café is still climbing out of the recession. Recently, my business has started to pick up, but I still have to budget conservatively.

I've never been inside a prison before. I'm kind of nervous about going but at least Mike will be with me. Of course, he's not allowed to talk to Amy in an official capacity. We'll have to pose as a couple of friends or relatives of hers. Hopefully, she'll agree to see us.

Chapter 8

Mike

Yesterday Edith and I drove to the prison in Hendersonville. I had been in the men's penitentiary before but this was my first visit to the women's facility. I wasn't sure what to expect. I thought I should wear my uniform in case anyone gave us a hard time about trying to see Amy. Edith disagreed. She was afraid the uniform might scare Amy after her run-in with "the law." In the end, I decided she was right. Of course, as a law enforcement officer, I knew no one could visit a convict without the prisoner's permission. So, I did my homework.

First, I found out who Amy's trial attorney was. I discovered that—because good ol' generous Hank refused to enlist an attorney for his only daughter, and because Stella couldn't afford to pay for one—Amy was appointed a lawyer by the court system. Her name is Thomason—Gloria Thomason. I scheduled a meeting with her to discuss Amy's case. She seemed cavalier about the whole matter. She said because Amy had been caught in the act, it was nearly impossible to build a case for her defense. It took the entire hour, but I finally convinced her that some details about the case raised suspicion and were worth re-investigating. Conveniently, I failed to mention my questioning was not the result of an official police investigation. Ms. Thomason agreed to contact Amy, and she convinced her to talk to me.

Throughout the thirty-minute drive to Hendersonville, I could tell Edith was nervous, so I tried to reassure her. We talked about what questions we would ask. Both of us hoped the young woman might trust us enough to offer information that could help her case. Edith reminded me it might take more than one visit before Amy would feel comfortable enough to speak openly. After all, as far as she was concerned, we were just a couple of indifferent strangers. "Before we can begin to build her trust," Edith reminded me, "we must first establish a relationship. We must convince Amy we care about both her and her mother." I was beginning to appreciate Edith's common sense.

I pulled my truck into the parking lot of the unimposing structure. The detention center was not surrounded by a tall chain link fence and topped with swirls of barbed wire like in the movies. I expected to see a gate with guards posted. Instead, only the walls of a modern brick building separated some two hundred female prisoners from their former lives of freedom but—more importantly for many of them—from their children. It's hard to believe so many women could have gotten mixed up in a life of crime. As a law enforcement officer, I've learned that female murderers, especially serial killers, are extremely rare. Women get locked up mostly for crimes like petty theft, shoplifting, or passing bad checks. Typically, violent female offenses result from self-defense—most commonly in response to years of cruel mental and/or physical abuse.

We had come during the daily visiting hour with proper authorization, but Amy could still change her mind and refuse to see us. Once inside we had to check in at the front desk and deposit our belongings in a basket. Next, a guard ushered us down a long corridor and into a waiting area. Dozens of visitors—husbands, boyfriends, and children, I assumed—were gathering there. Rather than the somber atmosphere we had expected, we found the visitors interacting with chatter and even laughter—more like one would expect at a family reunion. It put us somewhat at ease. Finally, our names were called over a loud speaker. We passed through a metal door and a metal detector. When the first door clanged shut behind us, Edith jumped. I could tell she was growing nervous as we approached the second door. She looked at me like she wanted to turn and go home. I placed my hand on her back and ushered her through the second door. As many times as I had been inside prisons, I never got used to the eerie, metallic sound of that second door locking me away from the outside world.

Edith and I wondered if we would recognize Amy from three-year-old newspaper clippings. We needn't have worried. She was the last prisoner to enter the room just beyond that wall of glass. Despite her forlorn expression, the young woman was still quite pretty, even without a drop of makeup. She looked very young and thin. Her long blonde hair was frizzy but looked clean and freshly brushed. I was mesmerized by her child-like appearance.

I raised my hand to elicit Amy's attention and remained standing until she reached our cubicle. She hesitated a moment, studying us, before she picked up the phone. Edith and I gingerly shared the filthy phone on our side of the partition. I spoke first. "Miss Leonard?"

"Yes, I'm Amy Leonard, Sergeant Travers. Who's this?" She was referring to Edith, of course.

"This is my friend, Edith Bowman. Your mother works for her." She stared at us with suspicion.

"My mother. You mean she's still alive?" she asked, bitterly.

"Yes. Why wouldn't she be?"

"I've been here for three years without a word from her, so I figured my father must have finally killed her."

"I knew it!" exclaimed Edith. "I knew he was beating her."

"Did he beat you, Amy?" I asked.

"Every chance he got." she growled resentfully. "He hated me from the day I was born."

"Why?" asked Edith.

"Because he was strung out on booze and crack and because I wasn't his precious Henry."

"The son who died?"

"Yeah."

"Did you do drugs, Amy?"

"Me? Hell, no!"

"Then, why were you buying them?"

"Listen, what's this about? I'm a felon—tried and convicted—doing my time. What's the point of digging up the past? I just want to serve my sentence, finish my education, and get out of this God-forsaken place."

"To tell the truth, we're worried about your mother. We think her life may be in danger."

"Of course her life's in danger. She's living with a monster and so is my baby girl, as far as I know."

"Baby? What baby? You have a child?"

"She ain't—isn't—a baby anymore... probably wouldn't even know her own mama. Her name's Jodie. She'd be six now."

"And you think she's living with your parents? Are you sure?"

"I ain't—I'm not—sure of anything. Like I said, I haven't seen or heard from either of them in three years. Jodie could be in the welfare system for all I know. She'd be better off, that's for sure." Her eyes filled with tears which she wiped away roughly, sadness quickly turning to anger. "I didn't even get to say good-bye. I never saw my little girl after I was arrested... not once." Edith started to reach toward the glass partition like she wanted to touch the young woman. From Amy's body language, I got the impression she would have pulled away even if the glass hadn't separated them.

"Listen, Amy," I said, trying to sound as innocuous as possible, "we think there's something suspicious about your case. We aren't convinced of your guilt."

"So? What difference does it make?"

"If I can persuade my captain to reopen your case, there's a chance you could be released early."

"Then what? Are you gonna make my daddy love me? Are you gonna save my mama from being killed by him? Are you gonna find my Jodie? Are we gonna live happily ever after?" She was shouting now but nobody noticed her tirade. When she started to hang up, I realized my chances of winning her trust were fading quickly. Fortunately, Edith intervened.

"Wait, Amy, please." Edith said. Amy froze, staring at the counter with the phone dangling from her hand. Then, she brought it to her ear once more. "We can't make any promises but we want to try," Edith continued. "We think your mother is just as much a victim as you are of your father's illness or evil or whatever it is."

She looked at us again, her eyes filled with anger. "She never stood up to him. She never tried to stop him. She let him beat her and me and my Jodie, too."

"She's trapped, Amy," Edith said. "Your mother is a good, decent woman who's trapped in an abusive relationship. We can't change that or anything else without your help. May we come again?"

"But why? Why do you even care?" When she had pulled the phone closer to her ear again I allowed myself a glimmer of hope. Now, Edith needed to talk fast.

"We don't expect you to trust us, Amy," Edith continued, trying to connect with the woman's downcast eyes. "You don't even know us. But what can it hurt to let us try to help? We think you were convicted unjustly and we think your mother is in mortal danger—maybe your daughter, too. Isn't that enough reason?"

"Jodie might already be dead for all I know." Amy buried her face in her free hand and finally gave in to tears. "My beautiful baby girl," she mumbled through sobs. "He always hated her. I have terrible nightmares about what he must be doing to her without me there to protect her."

"Let us see what we can do, Amy, okay?" Edith said.

"Knock yourselves out," she said with a shrug, then making eye contact, she added, "but if my baby's dead I don't want to know about it. You got that?"

Suddenly, coming over the phone, a recording warned us our time was almost up.

"We have only a few minutes remaining. I need to know one thing before we leave," I said.

"What's that?"

"Did Hank make you buy his drugs? Is that why you were meeting the dealer?"

"Every freakin' Saturday since I turned twelve," she said, disgust filling her voice. "If I came home without 'em, I got whipped till my skin was raw and bloody and sent back out till I found some."

"And it continued until you finally got caught in a raid," Edith added.

"That's about the size of it. That's what I told the police and that worthless lawyer, too. But nobody believed me. Nobody even checked my story, as far as I can tell."

"It's time somebody did," I said.

"When you're poor, folks just assume you're trash. They throw you on the garbage heap and forget about you."

"We'll be back, Amy. Don't give up hope, okay?" The young woman sighed heavily. She roughly wiped her dripping eyes and nose with the backs of her hands, and stood to leave.

"In my world," she said, dejectedly, "hope and disappointment are kissin' cousins."

"We'll come back next week," Edith assured her.

"Suit yourselves."

"Oh, one more thing," said Edith. "I bought you something, but they wouldn't let me give it to you. I'll have to mail it."

"What is it?"

"Just some girlie stuff I thought you might like."

"Thanks," she said. She appeared more embarrassed than grateful. Then, turning to join the line of orange jump-suited women, Amy disappeared through the heavy door, and returned to her dull gray home-away-from-home.

The drive back to town was quiet for the first ten minutes or so, with Edith and me each lost in our own deep thoughts about what we had witnessed. Edith was first to break the silence. "What do you think, Mike? Is there any chance at all of helping that poor broken girl?"

"Somebody has to and it might as well be us. And what about *her* little girl? *That* was a shock! I had no idea there was a child."

"I'd say she's our priority, wouldn't you?"

"Absolutely! Where could she be? Has Stella ever mentioned a child?"

"No, but Stella is very private, as you know. Let's see. Amy said she would be six. That means she'd be in school."

"She couldn't be living with Hank and Stella, surely. Unless that's the reason Stella has to be home by four-thirty every day."

"I can nose around the elementary school near their house. Regina—the counselor—would know if the child goes there. Jodie, she said, right?"

"Yes, Jodie Leonard, I assume. It would seem that Amy and the child's father never married."

"How awful for a young child to be separated from her mother all these years," I said. "She probably barely remembers her. Do you want me to drop you at the café?"

"Yes, thanks. Dinner prep will be underway and I'm short-handed. Will I see you later, Mike?"

"You bet. I'll be in at the usual time."

"Chicken Cacciatore is the special tonight."

"Yum!" As I let Edith out in front of her café, it occurred to me that we make a good team, Edith and I. I found myself wondering why a fine-looking woman like her had never married.

Jodie

My back and legs are still hurting where Hank hit me yesterday. I reckon that's the worst beating yet. My legs have marks all over them and my back feels like it's broke every time I move. He hurt Stella real bad, too, knocked a tooth plum out of her head. Blood went flying everywhere.

Later somebody came to the front door. I heard Stella talking like everything was fine. I wanted to scream and holler but I was too scared. I knew Hank might wake up and start hitting us again. I don't know why he gets so mad. I try to be good and quiet. I try not to make any trouble. I don't know how to make him stop and Stella don't either, I reckon. I remember he always got mad at Amy, too, but she fought back. One time she hollered real loud at him and throwed a hairbrush at him. He grabbed her and whipped her good and called her names like "filthy whore," but she kept fighting the whole time and biting him on his arms. Maybe she got mad once too many times and he killed her. Maybe Stella tells me she's alive so I won't be sad. If he killed Mama, I hope he kills me next 'cause if he kills Stella first... I just don't know what.

On the television box, the police helps people. Why doesn't Stella ask the police to help us? Seems like they could put Hank in the jail so he'd stop hurting us. When I get growed up, I'm gonna be a police lady and stop mean men like Hank hurting people like my mama and Stella, too. I'll shoot 'em dead with my police gun so they can't hurt anybody anymore. Then I'll go to Target or Walmart and get everything we need to be happy, especially lots and lots of food.

Edith

Our visit to the prison was quite an eye-opener. All those women locked away from their families. It's so sad. What could make a woman commit a crime she knows will take her away from her children? It's not natural— which makes me think she would have to be desperate somehow... or forced into crime like Amy Leonard was. My heart goes out to that girl. Not only is she locked up for a crime she was forced to commit, but she lost all contact with her mother and daughter. How tragic! It's no wonder she's so cynical. Life has never given her anything except a huge kick in the teeth. How can she trust anybody when everyone in her life has failed her? How can she ever trust the justice system? I hope Mike and I can do something for her. She needs a break, that's for sure.

The more I get to know Mike, the more I realize what a great guy he is. He seems to have the perfect balance of compassion and toughness, like Charlie did. I like those qualities in a man, and I like the way Mike handled Amy. With a few more visits, I think she might start to trust us. I surely hope we don't disappoint her.

At some point, I'll tell Stella about our visit, but for now I need to complete her training so she can earn more money. I figured a way to pay her the wage increase without Hank knowing about it and without getting in trouble with the IRS. She'll still get a check with the usual amount. Then, I'll direct-deposit a bonus check into a new personal account.

I hope Mike has some luck finding Amy's little girl. How tragic it would be if the child has been in the foster care system all this time or even worse, if she's dead. I doubt she could have been adopted without Amy's permission, but what do I know about the legal rights of incarcerated parents?

Chapter 9

Mike

I've been trying to locate Amy's kid, but there doesn't seem to be any record of a Jodie Leonard, at least not in the immediate area. Regina says there's no one by that name attending the elementary school, and social services has no record of a child by that name, either. In fact, a record of her birth is not even on file at Frye Hospital or at City Hall. It's a mystery. I was beginning to wonder if Amy fabricated the whole story. Then I remembered what Andy said about her dropping out of school suddenly in the middle of her senior year. It certainly could be explained by a pregnancy. Maybe Mrs. Rutherford—the high school counselor—can verify it. I'll pay her a visit tomorrow.

If Jodie is living with her grandparents, Joe and Greg saw no signs of a child when they went to the residence. I guess it's time to have a talk with Stella. Edith thinks she might get nervous and bolt if we ask too many questions, but I suspect the pay increase will help to hold her here for a while. The fact is, we can't begin to help her—or Amy either—without more information. Edith seems to be good at asking questions in a non-threatening way. I'll leave that inquisition up to her.

In the meantime, I think I'll take a leap of faith and ask Edith out on a real date. I already know her better than I knew Libby the day we got married. What a fool I was to marry a woman I knew would break my heart… and my wallet! I was too young to think beyond my raging hormones and manly pride. If I marry again—and I'm not saying I will—it'll be for the right reasons. Edith is the finest woman I've ever met and we get along really well. Of course, it doesn't hurt that she's attractive—not glamorous like Libby—but good-looking in a wholesome way. I like her eyes. They seem honest. She has a nice body, too. She runs a few times a week and it shows. I like a woman who takes care of her health.

What if she turns me down? What if she just wants to remain friends? She's not a flirty kind of woman. That makes it hard to tell if she likes me or anyone else in a romantic way. Oh, crap! What if she's gay? I never thought of that before, but it could explain why she's thirty-five or so and never married. Come on Mike! You're letting your imagination run rampant because you're scared of rejection. Just do it. You'll never know unless you try.

Edith

When Mike came in for breakfast yesterday, he seemed a bit skittish. I asked him if anything was wrong but he said he was fine… just a little preoccupied. We discussed "the case"—I admit this business with Stella has me starting to feel like a bona fide detective. "Did you talk to Mrs. Rutherford?" I asked.

"What? Oh yeah. I sure did," he answered, acting strangely anxious. "Wait till you hear what I found out. It doesn't make any sense."

"Hold that thought, Mike. I need to get Stella started on her next task in the office. Also, I want to make sure she's not within earshot. I'll be right back." When I returned to the counter Mike was a million miles away working on his second cup of coffee.

"What's up with you today, Mike? You don't seem like yourself."

"Listen, Edith, I need to ask you a question, okay?"

"Sure. What is it?"

"Well, um, I was just wondering."

"For heaven's sake, spit it out before you have a stroke."

"Okay, okay. Here it is. I was wondering if you'd go out with me… on a date, I mean."

"Is that all? Is that why you've been acting like you have ants in your pants this morning? Of course, I'll go out with you."

"You will? Honest?"

"Honest. I must say it took you long enough to ask." I was smiling broadly, but Mike just looked immensely relieved and ever so serious. It was comical to watch this big, sturdy police officer acting like a jittery schoolboy. Because I didn't want to embarrass him, though, I restrained my amusement and quickly asked, "Where and when?"

He was obviously relieved. "I thought we might have dinner at that new French restaurant by the golf course, Bonvivant, and then take in a movie. How's Saturday night?"

"Perfect," I replied. "Now tell me what Mrs. Rutherford said."

"What? Oh. Well, she was pretty tight-lipped at first—privacy issues and all that—but when I mentioned I could get a warrant she finally revealed that Amy was, indeed, pregnant when she dropped out of school."

"Then, what happened to the baby? Where is Jodie now?"

"She had no idea. All she could say for sure was that Amy got a job some months later and earned her GED." Clearly Mike was more relaxed now and able to focus on our conversation.

"I think it's time to talk to Stella. If we can reassure Amy that her child is safe and happy, it'll raise her spirits and give her a reason to help us mount a new defense. I think we're getting closer to convincing Captain Howard to reopen the case."

"Great. Do you want to talk to her now?" I asked.

"I've got to get to work, but I was thinking it might be best if you spoke to her alone. She trusts you and she doesn't even know me. Besides, my uniform might frighten her."

"I agree. I'll talk to her today. I'll see you later. And, Mike?"

"Yeah?"

"I'm looking forward to our date."

"Me, too," he said as he finally smiled.

After the lunch-hour rush, I went to my office carrying a turkey sandwich with chips and a sweet tea for Stella. She was fixated intently on the computer screen. Only two days earlier I had shown her how to use the Quicken program, and already she was a whiz at it.

"My goodness. Is it lunchtime already?" she asked as she glanced up from her work.

"Actually, it's almost two. I thought you might be getting hungry."

"Yes, Ma'am… I mean Edith, I sure am! Thank you. I'll just eat while I finish this report."

"Take a break, Stella. I'd like to talk to you while you eat if that's okay."

"Of course. Did I do somethin' wrong?"

"Not at all. In fact, I'm amazed at how quickly you're picking up on the business end of things. You're doing a great job, Stella, and I feel like you'll be ready, very soon, to act as assistant manager."

"You won't leave me alone just yet, will you?"

"No, of course not. We'll work side-by-side until you feel completely confident."

"Oh, good. I ain't—I'm not—ready to take charge of the whole café yet." She sat back in my desk chair and began to eat her sandwich. I noticed that since receiving a promotion she had become conscious of her language and was obviously trying to improve her speech. This woman's strength and resilience never ceased to amaze me.

"What did you want to talk about?" she asked.

I started cautiously. "I've noticed that… often you have bruises and other signs of injury."

"Yeah, I'm right clumsy, especially with this here cane. I fall down a lot." She had stopped eating and now sat forward in the chair. She placed her sandwich on the plate, lowered her gaze, and began wringing her hands in her lap.

"Stella, I know Hank is abusing you, and I want to help if I can."

"Can't nobody help," she muttered under her breath, overcome with embarrassment.

"Stella, there's always a way out of a bad situation, but sometimes we need a little help. A woman in your… circumstances… needs a friend—someone she can talk to—someone she can trust. Do you trust me?" I closed the door so we could have some privacy and pulled a chair next to my desk facing her.

"I, I think so." She looked so frightened and fragile. My heart went out to her. I wished she would just tell me everything and get it over with. Of course, I understood why she felt hesitant to share her story. Mike had explained the psychology of the typical battered woman which prompted me to conduct my own research on the Internet. I said a silent prayer that Stella would feel safe with me and that God would help me listen in a way to put her at ease.

"Hank ain't—isn't—a bad man, leastwise he didn't start out that way."

"What happened to change him?"

"I done something terrible back when we was first married and he ain't… hasn't… ever forgiven me."

"What could you have done to deserve his hurting you all these years?"

"I… I killed our little boy, our precious Henry."

"You had a son?" I asked, feigning ignorance so she would elaborate.

"Henry were… was… only five years old. He fell out a window and broke his neck."

"But that was an accident, Stella. Surely you can't believe you killed him."

"Hank blames me, always has, and I shoulda been watchin' more careful. I shouldn't have left him alone like that." Now—with her hands covering her face—she began crying. Gently, I touched her shoulder.

"Stella, it wasn't your fault. It was an accident. It could have happened to any mother anywhere. Hank has no right to blame you or abuse you because he can't handle his own grief and anger." Suddenly, she took a deep breath, raised her head and covered her mouth to mute a horrific gut-wrenching cry. She collapsed into my arms and sobbed and sobbed. I held her for several minutes and let her cry until she was spent. I cried, too—not only for her and Henry but also for the baby boy Charlie and I lost to miscarriage. There we sat, wrapped in each other's arms, sharing the unique sisterhood of maternal loss.

Finally, Stella looked up, pulled a tissue from her pocket, blew her nose and proclaimed, "Blessed Mary! I never cried for my Henry before. That's the first time—the very first time… and it felt so good. Thank you, Edith. Thank you for lettin' me cry for my dead baby and for saying it weren't my fault. I always blamed myself. I always thought Hank had the right to beat me because I killed his son."

"He was *your* son, too. There is no justification for abuse, Stella! None! Do you hear me? Hank has no right to hit you."

"But what can I do to make it stop?" she sniffed. "He gets so mad, especially when he's drunk and drugged-up."

"I have some ideas, but first I need to ask you another question."

"What is it?" she asked, her voice shaky and weak. I hesitated for a moment, fearing I might send her back to her life of secrecy, but finally, I just blurted it out.

"Where's your grandchild, Stella? Where's Jodie?" Seeing the look of shock and terror on her face, I knew I may have taken my inquiry too far. I risked causing her to shut me out once more.

"What do you mean?" She stood, grabbed her cane and started pacing. "What are you talking about? I ain't got no grandchild. Like I said, my son died when he was only five. I don't know what you're talkin' about." As upset as she was with this line of questioning, I realized I had opened a can that couldn't be put back on the shelf. I decided to press further.

"Stella, I know about Amy, your daughter, and I know she had a child."

"I thought you said I could trust you when all the time you been snooping into my past!" she shouted indignantly. "How can I trust somebody who's been prying into my personal life?" Just then, Louie came to the door and knocked.

"Edith, is everything all right in there?" he called through the closed door.

"Yes, Louie. Everything's fine," I answered. "I'll be out in a few minutes."

"Okay, but let me know if you need anything."

"I will. Thanks." Then turning back to Stella, I declared, "Stella, I'm your employer. I have the right to investigate you or any other employee. You can trust that my motives are honorable. I only want to help if I can."

"How can you help? How can anybody help? My Amy's been rottin' in that prison cell for three long years, and Hank won't let me see her or talk to her or nothin'. She's all alone in this world, and it's his fault she got sent away to begin with."

"I know, Stella. I know all about it. I know about Hank's drug problem and I know about Amy's incarceration. None of that is your fault, either. You are not to blame. You must believe me."

"I don't know what to believe. I just know I ain't—haven't—seen or talked to Amy in three long years. Not once."

"Stella, I've been to see your daughter." I was really pushing the envelope now, but somehow, I thought I needed to get as much information as I could while I had the chance.

"What? You seen my Amy? Why? How? Is she okay? She hates me. I know she hates me and I can't blame her. She must think I deserted her. How you gonna help my Amy when nobody else ever did?"

"I know somebody who can help. His name is Mike Travers and he's a police sergeant. You know the cop who comes in for breakfast every day?"

"Yeah, I know the one, but what can he do? Can he get Amy outta jail?"

"It's possible, but first you must tell me about Jodie."

"I can't," she whispered as she sat again.

"Yes, you can and you *must* if you want Mike's help and mine. I know all of this has been upsetting. We can talk again tomorrow, but you must promise not to do anything crazy—like run away."

"Ha! Where would I go and how would I get there?"

"Please, just trust me and trust Mike. He's a stand-up guy and he cares. I promise we can fix this situation together, but we have to be careful not to make Hank suspicious while we work out the details. We don't want to make things harder for you—and this is important—if at any time, you think your life is in danger, I want you to call Mike at this number." I pulled a Post-it note off the dispenser on my desk. I wrote Mike's cell phone number on it and handed it to Stella. "Do you promise?"

"Yeah, okay, I promise," she agreed weakly, but I wasn't convinced she would follow through.

"Now we had both better get back to work," I said and stood to leave the room.

"Edith?" she asked sheepishly, drying her red eyes and nose with her napkin. "Do you think Sergeant Travers could get me into the prison to see Amy? She probably don't want to see me but I just need to lay eyes on my girl."

"I'm sure he can. I'll see what I can arrange."

"Hank can't know," she added, fearfully.

"Of course not. Mike can take you during working hours and Hank will never suspect a thing." As I left Stella sitting at my desk, I couldn't help but think about the many women who spend every minute of their lives in fear. According to what I had been reading, Stella was only one among millions. Even if Mike and I succeeded in helping her escape her wretched life, who would help the others? For a moment, hopelessness overwhelmed me. At least I had made significant progress with Stella. She had actually admitted to being abused. That was a huge step forward. I decided to drop the subject of her granddaughter for now. I could only hope Mike had made some headway in locating the child.

Chapter 10

Mike

I thought Saturday night would never come. I was like a nervous teenager getting ready for the prom—which is ridiculous for a grown man who has been married and divorced. I was fairly popular in high school and college, not because I had an outgoing personality—in fact, I've always been kind of shy—but because I was a football jock. I had no trouble getting dates or being invited to parties then. But this was different. *Edith* was different. If I had to describe her, I'd say she's a real woman who lives life authentically. She doesn't try to impress other people, and she accepts them just the way they are without judgment. I've known for a while I liked her, but when I saw how she handled herself with Amy Leonard in that prison, I realized I was falling in love with her. If this date is to go well, I must be careful not to try too hard. Edith will see right through me.

We decided to meet at the restaurant. I arrived first, wearing what I like to call my date-night uniform: blue Oxford shirt and yellow tie with khakis and a navy sport coat. The maître d' ushered me to a table on the back terrace overlooking the golf course. On this glorious spring evening a gentle breeze made the candles flicker, casting wavy shadows across the tables. The pergola-covered terrace was surrounded by an array of spring blossoms that gave off a sweet fragrance with every gust of wind. Just beyond the ninth fairway, the sunset painted the horizon a deep pink, and I found myself wishing Edith would hurry so as not to miss the show.

As I glanced inside the restaurant, I noticed the maître d' was leading a very attractive brunette in my direction. Although a shadow obscured her face, I could see her slender, athletic frame was draped in a sexy red number. She wore black high heels and carried a black shawl and bejeweled purse. *Wow!* I thought. *Now, there's a sight to get a man's blood pumping!* Aware that I was gawping, I turned back to the golf course to admire the final moments of that beautiful sunset. Suddenly I realized the woman looked familiar. She was so glamorous that for a fleeting moment I thought of Libby. *What the hell is she doing here? Oh, my freakin'...*

"Good evening, Mike," the goddess said. Was she speaking to me? I tried to stand but my legs decided they didn't want to support me. I leaned on the table for reinforcement. Fortunately, the maître d' held her chair and draped a napkin across her lap as she sat. With my jaw nearly lying on the table, I managed to keep my drool from spilling onto the linen tablecloth.

"Edith, is that you?" I asked, mesmerized by the transformation.

"Well, if it isn't, I just stole Edith Bowman's car and clothes."

"But you look... I've never seen you look so..."

"What? You thought I was going to wear my uniform and hairnet on our date?"

"No, but... wow! You look gorgeous."

"Thank you. You look very nice, too."

"It's just that I didn't expect... I guess I've never seen you dressed up before. I really like your hair loose like that... not that I don't like it pulled back. It's just that... wow!"

"So, I take it you approve?"

"Oh, yeah," I sighed. I was making a complete fool of myself. I saw it happening like a movie flashing before me, but couldn't seem to stop my spiral into idiocy. Fortunately, the sommelier arrived to take our wine order, affording me a chance to swallow, breathe, and regain what little dignity I could salvage. From Edith's expression, I could tell she was entertained thoroughly by my awkward discomfort.

"Okay, I hope you're satisfied with your ability to turn a grown man into a blithering idiot, Ms. Bowman," I said, once we were alone again.

"Oh, yes, quite satisfied," she said, smugly, fluttering her mascaraed eyelashes for effect. Edith had never worn mascara to work that I could recall. It was just enough to enhance her sparkling eyes and long lashes but not so much as to look slutty. "Hey Mike," she whispered. "This place looks really expensive. Are you sure you can afford it?"

"Nice way to kill the mood, Sexy." We had recovered our usual, playful banter, and thankfully, I was beginning to feel more relaxed. "Actually, a grateful citizen gave me a generous gift certificate for helping her mother after a nasty fall. Unless you decide to order Dom Pérignon and lobster, I should only have to pay the tip and sales tax."

"Oh, good. I wouldn't be able to enjoy the evening if I thought it was going to strap you." That was Edith, always thinking of other people. We sat in silence for a few minutes as we looked over the menus, but I couldn't resist peeking over the top of mine at the vision of loveliness sitting across from me.

I didn't know what half the stuff on the menu was, but Edith had studied French cuisine in culinary school. She recommended a fish dish that turned out to be scrumptious even if I still can't pronounce the name.

We conversed with ease throughout dinner—which was delicious—mainly about Stella and Amy. Edith asked if I could arrange for Stella to see Amy. Of course, I agreed. Both of us were baffled by the lack of information about Amy's daughter. Where could she be? Edith said Stella shut down when she mentioned Jodie. So, she thought it best to not push too hard. She was hoping I had made a discovery. Unfortunately, I had to admit my inquiries had turned up nothing. I promised to keep searching until I found something—anything—that might provide a clue as to the child's whereabouts.

Finally, over digestifs, I got up the nerve to pose the question that had crossed my mind more than once, "How is it that a beautiful, intelligent woman like you never married?"

"Thanks for the compliment, but who says I never married?"

"Well, I just thought… are you divorced, too?"

"No, Mike. My husband died. I'm a widow."

"I'm sorry. I didn't know. You never said anything."

"It happened a while back, but it's still a little hard to talk about it."

"We don't have to."

"No, it's okay. His name was Charlie. Charles Bowman. We were married only two years when we found out he was sick. Cancer. How does a fit twenty-five-year-old man end up with terminal cancer? I've never figured out that one, but I guess if I had I'd be rich and famous, wouldn't I?" she said, cynically. I knew her questions were rhetorical, and I could see the asking caused Edith great pain. I remained silent while she talked about her one great love. It's a fact that we humans tend to venerate the dead, but the Charlie she described sounded like someone who could have been my best friend, a real swell guy. He also sounded like a man I could never have competed with for Edith's love.

"We had just discovered I was pregnant when…"

"Wait! You and Charlie had a child? You're full of surprises, Edith."

"No, I lost the baby after four months. It was a boy. Then Charlie took a turn for the worse, and within a year of his diagnosis, he was gone. It was like God was playing one cruel joke on me after another."

"Oh, Edith, I'm sorry." I said, instinctively covering her hand with mine. "How did you manage to survive so much tragedy?"

"For a while, I didn't. For many months, I could barely function. I wondered if I'd ever pull out of it."

"How did you?"

"I'm not sure I'll ever get over the losses, but after a while I had to make the decision to either live or die. I started going back to church and praying again. My church had a bereavement group that I attended for a while. We shared our stories with each other and learned about the various stages of grief. Finally, I realized God had been with me through all of them. I began to surrender my pain and loss to God and ask for the strength to recover. That was seven years ago, and today my life is good."

"Thanks for telling me," I said. "It must be hard to talk about it."

"Yeah, but it helps, too. Thanks for listening. Now tell me about Mike Travers." There wasn't much to tell that Edith didn't already know about me. The whole town knew about my brief, embarrassing marriage to Libby. What I wanted to show Edith was how much I had changed since then—how much I had matured.

We left the restaurant, walking hand-in-hand, and it felt right. The evening was so pleasant that we decided to skip the movie and stroll down by the lake. Oh, man! I was falling hard and I hoped she was, too. As we sat on a bench overlooking the marina I wanted to grab her and smother her in kisses. The mood seemed perfect but I couldn't risk scaring her off by moving too fast. After all, technically-speaking it was only our first date. For a few minutes, we sat in silence watching the golden moonlight dance across the water. A cool breeze rustled the newly sprouted leaves that hung above our heads and caused the sailboat riggings to clang against their masts. Just as I was planning my one restrained good-night kiss, Edith turned to me and asked, "Well, Sergeant, are you going to kiss me or what?" That was all the invitation I needed.

"It sure would be a waste of a perfect romantic setting if I didn't," I said, taking her in my arms. I tried not to act overly eager, though our kisses felt to me like a homecoming celebration. At that moment, I knew for sure I wanted Edith to be my wife.

Stella

Since talking to Edith, I'm feeling confused and kind of scared, even though I think she wants to help. I ain't sure how much to say one way or another. I can't tell her about Jodie because if she tells that cop how my precious grand-baby is being treated, he'll be obliged to report it. Then Jodie'll get taken away and I might never see her again. It makes me sick every time I see her alone in that room day after day, wearin' that thin dress and strapped to the bed so she can't hardly move. The child needs sunshine and runnin' around. She needs more food than Hank'll let me give her, and she needs to be in school, learnin' to read and write. She needs her mama's hugs and toys to play with. She can't hardly talk and she's six years old now. She talked real good before Amy got took away. I could tell she was smart just like her mama. I gotta work out a plan to get us both outta that house and far away from Hank. I only hope one day Jodie--and her mama, too--can forgive me for allowin' her to suffer all this time. Maybe I should let them authorities take her away. She'd have a better life with a foster family, that's for sure. But she's *my* family and I love her. I want her and me and Amy to be together again... to start over someplace new. If *my* mama was still livin' she'd take Jodie till I could make a proper home for us. I ain't got nobody to turn to except Edith.

Edith says I'm doing real good learnin' my new job. She thinks I'm smart. Imagine that! She says my extra pay will start next week. She wants me to leave work early on Friday and go by the bank to set up a checking account in just my name. She says Hank won't be able to touch that money. He won't even know about it because she's paying me by direct-deposit.

Sergeant Travers promised to take me to the prison over in Hendersonville to see Amy. I'm excited about that but nervous and scared, too. What if Amy don't want to see me? What if she gets mad and starts yellin'? I wouldn't blame her one bit. I'm scared she won't ever stop hatin' me. Maybe it's better not to know. Oh, God! What if she asks about Jodie? Of course, she will. What do I say that ain't a lie? What do I say that won't get the sergeant to snoopin' around? Every time I think maybe things could get better, another stumblin' block plops down in my path. Sometimes I wonder why I ever got born into this world. I wonder why life has to be so blamed hard. I best not get my hopes up. It ain't never helped before, just made me fall farther and land harder.

Edith

Well, well! Who knew Sergeant Travers was a good kisser? After Charlie died I was sure I'd never fall in love again. Ours was one of those once-in-a-lifetime romances, I thought. After his death—when the fog of grief finally began to lift—I prepared to live the rest of my life alone. The café kept me plenty busy—plus I had my church activities, my running buddies, and my book club. My brother's kids, despite living in the next state, helped to fill the void left by childlessness. It seemed life could be full even in the absence of a love interest. Then along came Mike… a great guy who's easy to talk to, but just a friend for several years. Last night changed all that. When he took me in his arms down by the lake, I realized it might be possible to experience the blessing of more than one soulmate in a lifetime. I could tell he felt the connection too. We're going out again next weekend. I'll see Mike every day from now until then, but my heart skips a beat whenever I think about spending another evening alone with him.

I wish Stella could be given a second chance at love. Hank has her so beaten down she doesn't think anybody could care for her. I believe she could be attractive with a decent haircut and a little makeup. The first order of business is to get her away from that abusive addict.

I hope Mike locates Stella's granddaughter soon, so at least *they* can be reunited. She doesn't seem to have a clue as to the girl's whereabouts. Mike said he would check with CPS this week to see if the child is being fostered. How strange that he can't find a record of her birth. Hmm. I wonder if Amy left town to have her baby. Maybe Mike should expand his search.

Chapter 11

Mike

I am one lucky dude. Edith actually wants to go out with me again. And she initiated our first kiss. Wow! I think I saw fireworks exploding over the lake last night—or were they inside my head? I couldn't sleep thinking about Edith and how much I want to be with her. When she walked into that restaurant looking like a fashion model—only better—I nearly dropped my teeth on the table. The best part is I knew I loved her before I saw her all glammed up. It's the exact opposite of my relationship with Libby—if you can call what we had a relationship. The difference between Edith and Libby is that Edith is a beautiful woman inside as well as outside. Sometimes I think hardship and tragedy shape people into stronger individuals—people with depth of character. I'm ready to ask her to marry me tomorrow, but I need to be careful not to scare her off by moving too fast. Also, I want to be established financially before I pop the question. Edith needs to know I'm responsible and dependable. I need to be able to offer her a home and a stable future. I haven't told her yet but I'm studying to make lieutenant. In just a few weeks I can take the exam. If I pass, I'll get promoted.

Speaking of hardship and tragedy, it seems that Stella Leonard has experienced enough tragedy for *two* lifetimes. The more I delve into her life the more questions surface. For instance, why can't I find her granddaughter? I've checked the birth (and death) records for the entire county and there's no sign of a Jodie Leonard anywhere. Edith said when she broached the subject with Stella, the woman refused to talk about her grandchild, like she was afraid. Is it possible Hank killed Jodie and disposed of her body? Even if that were the case it doesn't explain why there's no record of her birth.

My next strategy is to ask Captain Howard about setting up a sting operation to bust Hank for using illegal narcotics. We know he replenishes his supply every Saturday morning as soon as he cashes his paycheck (and Stella's). Now we need to find out where and from whom. If I were to trail him and gather evidence, even my eyewitness report of a deal wouldn't stand up in court. The captain would have to sanction it first. The problem is he's convinced Hank's suppliers were imprisoned with Amy. If Hank is involved with Juan Vasquez we could kill two birds with one stone. I may be able to convince the captain that nabbing Vasquez is worth the manpower expense for a stakeout.

Vasquez has escaped indictment again and again for years, allowing his lackeys to take the heat for him. He has brought millions of dollars' worth of drugs into our community and the surrounding towns. He has caused untold crime and created heartache for countless families. Everybody knows it. Yet nobody has been able to pin anything concrete on him. If we could trace Hank's activity to Vasquez and put him away the whole area—probably the whole state—would benefit and Captain Howard would surely receive a commendation. Unfortunately, Hank's transactions sound more like amateur stuff, like high school kids making a fast buck. I mean, who sells drugs on the street in broad daylight on Saturday morning?

In the meantime, I'm going to drive Stella to the prison to see Amy. Edith says she'll give Stella the time off work so Hank never has to know about it. Of course, there's a chance Amy will refuse to see her mother. She resents Stella for not contacting her before now. Hopefully I can convince Amy that Hank's threats and abuse are what kept her mother away.

Edith

When Mike stopped in for breakfast this morning, he seemed different. I guess I must have come across as different, too. As hard as I tried to act nonchalant, Saturday night's date had changed things between us. Let's face it. Our date had changed everything. As a result, we were both acting awkward and downright giddy. Despite the electrifying kiss we shared, neither of us had declared our love. This morning we were caught in limbo—somewhere between friendship and romance.

"G' mornin', Edith," he said. He had removed his hat and jacket and was taking his usual place at the counter. Was he avoiding eye contact?

"Good morning to you, Mike," I responded as I poured his coffee. "How are you today?"

"Fine. How are you?"

"I'm fine. Will you have the usual?"

"Sure, the usual's fine."

Oh, brother, I thought. *How are we supposed to move past this awkwardness? Okay, let's just dive in, address the elephant in the room, so to speak.*

"I really enjoyed our date, Mike. That restaurant was wonderful, wasn't it?"

"It sure was." *Did I hear a sigh?* "Maybe I'll get another gift certificate so we can afford to eat there again," he laughed.

"Or I could sell *my* restaurant to pay for two meals at Bonvivant," I joked. Finally, we were starting to relax and interact with our usual playfulness. I decided to prolong the subject of our date. "*After* dinner was nice too. What a beautiful evening by the lake."

"What a beautiful *woman* by the lake," he whispered, brushing my hand. As our eyes met, sparks flew across the counter, and I knew I was in love with this man.

"Why, Sergeant Travers, you do flatter a girl." As I turned toward the kitchen to check on his order, he took my hand and held it for a moment.

"It's not flattery, Edith. You *are* beautiful and I'm madly in love with you." Before I could respond, he released my hand and quickly added, "But don't worry. We can take it as slowly as you like. No pressure, okay?"

"Who says I want to take it slowly?" Finally, a broad grin released the tension in his sturdy jaw, and each of us knew where we stood with the other.

As Mike devoured his usual breakfast of eggs, bacon, and grits, the conversation turned to our topic of late. "Are you going to talk to Captain Howard today about setting up a drug bust?" I asked.

"Absolutely. I've been thinking a lot about the situation and I'm convinced Stella's life is in danger."

"I agree. The sooner we get Hank behind bars the better. What about Jodie? Do you have any leads on her whereabouts?"

"Nothing but dead ends. I hope to get to the social services office today to nose around."

"Good. Is there any way I can help?"

"Do you think you could talk to Stella again? Surely she must know where the child is."

"I'm sure she knows, but Hank has her threatened into silence. I'm convinced she lives in fear for her life every day. You should have seen her face when I asked about Jodie. She looked terrified. I'm afraid to press too hard, Mike."

"I know, but see if you can get her talking about the child before Amy's arrest. Maybe she'll let something slip."

"Okay, I'll see what I can do. I mean, what grandmother doesn't enjoy talking about her grandchild?"

"Right. I'd better be going. I want to catch the captain before he gets too busy."

"Mike, do you think Jodie's dead? If she is dead Amy won't have anything to live for. She won't have any reason to help her own case."

"Let's not give up hope just yet. By the way, did I tell you I'm studying for the lieutenant's exam?"

"No. That's wonderful. When is it?"

"Not for a couple of weeks. It'll take me that long to get through the manual."

"You'll do great. Will I see you for lunch?"

"Not today. I'll have to use my lunch hour to visit DSS."

"Tomorrow morning, then. Call me if you learn anything new."

"You bet." As I watched Mike depart for the station, a sense of peace washed over me. In that moment, I knew he and I were going to be together for the rest of our lives. Each of us could leave the past behind and start fresh as a couple. There's something to be said for mature love. Neither of us is a kid. We've had enough life experience to know what we want in a partner and what we want out of life. Speaking of kids, I wonder if Mike wants any. Since my biological clock is slowing down we should discuss that topic sooner rather than later. Listen to me. We've been on one date, and already I'm thinking about having his children.

Stella

I got my first extra paycheck this week. Edith's givin' me a hundred more every week. That's twice as much as I been gettin' in tips. If I save every cent, I should be able to get me and Jodie outta that house and away from Hank real soon. I went straight to the bank and opened an account just like Edith said I should. Hank won't know nothin' about it. I'm real tempted to buy more food with that money because Jodie don't get enough to eat. She ain't growin' proper, I know. That's another reason I got to hatch my plan soon.

In the café, they's a rack of pamphlets near the door. One day as I was leavin' work, I noticed a new one right there in the front of the rack. It told about a shelter for women and children like Jodie and me. Until I read that paper I didn't know what Hank did to me made me a "battered wife." I just knowed he got mad and beat me. I took the pamphlet on the bus with me and read the whole thing front-to-back. It said a battered woman is mostly someone who gets beat up by a man but not always. Sometimes she just gets yelled at or humiliated ("emotionally abused") by him. Well, I figured that must be me because Hank does both. It ain't right and it ain't legal, accordin' to the pamphlet. That really got me thinkin'. For a long time, I thought it was okay for him to do them things to me because he was my husband. I thought I deserved it for lettin' our baby fall to his death. It was Amy and Jodie that I wanted to protect from his hittin' and hollerin'.

The shelter, called Agape House, is like a real home, the pamphlet said, where women and children can live safely till they get on their feet. It didn't say where this Agape place is because if it did, the men—the abusers—would find it. It's somewhere in this here town. There's a number to call, and I memorized it so I could throw the paper away before I got home. I can't risk Hank findin' it. Maybe Jodie and me could live there at Agape House for a while, just till I get enough money saved for our own place.

I got to find a leather cutter or a saw or something to cut that strap offa Jodie's leg—something that won't take long to cut through it. I won't have much time while Hank's out gettin' his drugs or passed out from takin' 'em. If he catches me cuttin' that strap offa Jodie's leg, he'll kill me and her both. I got to be real careful not to disturb him. I know! A razor blade. That would cut through leather fast, I'll bet. I just have to find something to shove in between the strap and Jodie's leg so I don't cut her.

Then, I gotta get us both to the bus station somehow. Maybe Edith will take us. She said she wanted to help. No. I can't ask Edith. She'll tell Sergeant Travers and he'll have to report me for not takin' proper care of Jodie. I might even get charged with kidnapping. If Jodie gets took away from me I don't know what I'll do. I just couldn't take losin' another baby. No. I can't tell Edith. Tonight, after Hank falls asleep, I'll call that hotline number just to see what this shelter's all about and see if it's close enough for me to get us there.

63

Chapter 12

Mike

I spent my lunch hour at the social services office, combing their files from six years ago to the present. If Captain Howard discovered I was using my badge to do unauthorized investigating, he'd probably take it away. But there's something suspicious about this Leonard case. I can't rest until I sort it out. It's like Jodie Leonard just disappeared into thin air. There's no record of her entering the welfare system—at least not in *this* county. So, where is she? It's time for Edith to press Stella for more information. For Amy's sake, I hope that child is still alive.

I did make some headway with the captain this morning. He agreed to set up a stakeout at the Leonard place next Saturday morning. Two plain-clothes officers in an unmarked car will tail Hank in hopes of busting him on illegal drug possession. If we can put Hank behind bars it will be easier for Stella to escape his control. Howard doesn't think Hank is involved in the Vasquez ring—at least not directly—but he agrees any narcotics bust is a good bust, especially if high school kids are involved. There's a chance we can get them some help before they ruin their lives. Teenagers' brains aren't developed enough to comprehend the long-term consequences of their actions. They don't realize that once they turn eighteen they stand trial as adults and their records follow them forever. As a law enforcement officer, I feel an obligation to our young citizens to save them from immature actions that will have a negative impact on their futures. Parenting teenagers must be one of the hardest jobs in the world. Parents seem to get all the blame when their kids go wrong. But I don't think parents can do it alone, not today with so many harmful and tempting influences.

I wonder if Edith still wants to have children. After suffering the pain of miscarriage, she may be hesitant to try again. I couldn't fault her for it. If she decided to remain childless, I wouldn't let it stand in the way of marrying her. I've always wanted kids, though… lots of kids. I suppose we could adopt. Wow! We've had one date and already I'm planning marriage and kids. Mike Travers, you must be out of your mind.

Edith said she can spare Stella for a few hours Wednesday morning so I can take her to the prison. I have some comp hours coming from when I covered for Ted last month. The captain won't know how I'm spending my day-off, and we'll be back before Stella's quitting time.

I wonder how Amy will react to seeing her mother after nearly three years of no contact. She surely didn't have anything good to say about her. She blames Stella for everything that has gone wrong in her life, it seems. I wish Edith could go with us. I like the way she handled herself with Amy, but of course, somebody has to run the café while we're gone.

Stella

Yesterday, Sergeant Travers carried me over to the prison to see my girl. I was so nervous thinkin' about seein' her and about how she would act toward me, I couldn't say hardly a word the whole way to Hendersonville. The sergeant kept tryin' to get me to talk but I was scared to. I can see why Edith likes him. He's so kind and gentlemanly. He even opened the door to his truck for me to climb in. I ain't been that close to a nice man since I don't know when. Oh, there's some friendly men that comes into the café, but I figured maybe they was just nice in public like Hank can be when he needs to. I figured they probably went home and beat their wives, too.

When we got to the prison, I started to say I changed my mind, but then I remembered Sergeant Travers took a whole day off work and drove me all the way there. I had to go through with it. I took a deep breath and walked through the door. Everything was ugly battleship gray—the walls, the floors, the furniture, the guards' uniforms—everything. I couldn't believe my baby been livin' in that cold, lifeless place for three long years, especially bein' punished for somethin' she was forced to do. Amy's a smart girl, always did real good in school. She could've been a teacher or a doctor or anything she put her mind to. She could've went to college and got herself a good job and got away from Hank. Instead she took up with the first boy who said he loved her. I think she saw marriage as her way out, like I did. When she ended up pregnant, that boy denied bein' the father and off he went to college, leavin' her to raise their baby alone. Then she *was* stuck.

Hank wouldn't even let her go to the hospital to have the baby, made her give birth at home. He said we couldn't afford to pay for doctors and hospitals, especially to bring a bastard into the world. Hank never even looked at Jodie when she come out or paid her any mind as she grew into a sweet, bright little girl—except to holler at her and hit her when she didn't do what he wanted. Amy tried to stop him. She'd get between him and Jodie, lettin' him beat on her instead. She'd try to fight him off but them drugs made him too strong. It seemed like he was either passed out or a raving lunatic—nothin' in between.

After a while Amy got a part-time job at the Winn Dixie, but it didn't pay enough to support her and Jodie, plus she could only work when I was home to take care of the baby. Hank made her pay again and again for her mistake… made her feel like she weren't no better'n pond scum.

Amy never did learn the lesson Hank taught me all them years ago: either let him get it outta his system or fight back and risk bein' crippled or killed. When Amy was about seven, Hank pushed me so hard I fell over a chair and landed hard on my left side. I knowed my hip and arm was broke because of the horrible pain and because I heard snappin' sounds. Amy was hidin' behind the sofa—probably scared to death he'd come after her. He kept tellin' me to get up but I couldn't. I closed my eyes and just lay there, pretendin' to be unconscious. The pain was unbearable but I tried not to move or make a sound. Finally, Hank passed out on the sofa. I called to Amy real quiet so's I wouldn't wake her daddy. I told her to bring the phone as close as the cord would reach. Somehow, I dragged myself to it and called my mama to come get us. She took me to the hospital where I stayed for near a week and she took Amy home with her. She paid for the hospital, too. I told her I fell, accidental, but she knew the truth, I'm sure. When I got outta the hospital Amy and I spent two weeks with Mama. I wanted to stay there forever and not go back to Hank, but it were plain Mama already had the cancer that took her life and all of her savin's a few years later. Mama couldn't afford to pay for my physical therapy and I couldn't either. So, my hip never did heal right. That's why I have to use this here cane.

Well, anyway, Sergeant Travers and me, we got taken to a room in the prison with a whole lot of other visitors, some of 'em children. As we waited on one of them gray benches, I was shakin' and sweatin'. Finally, on the other side of a big window, some heavy metal doors slid open, and in flowed a dozen or so women wearing orange jumpsuits: white, black, mixed, young, and not-so young, tall and short, every one of 'em wearing them hollow eyes like they'd already lived two lifetimes. I looked at each face, knowin' I'd recognize my baby no matter how much she might've changed. There she was—my Amy. She looked thin, but oh so good! When she laid her eyes on me she acted like she'd seen a apparition. She gasped and covered her mouth as if she was about to upchuck. I wanted to run to her and smother her in hugs, but even if I coulda' reached through the glass and touched her, I could tell she was off-put.

"Shit!" she mouthed as she approached the table. Then, speaking into the phone, she asked, "What has he done to you?" Sergeant Travers stood to leave us alone, but I grabbed his sleeve. I just didn't think I could face my girl alone. What could I say to her that she would ever forgive me?

"I'll be right over there," the sergeant assured me, pointing to the bench where we first waited. "You two need some time to get re-acquainted." He was only a few feet away, but with the echoing din in that room, there's no way he coulda heard our conversation.

"Mama?" she cried, looking so sorrowful. She put one hand to the window and searched my face like she barely recognized me. Then the tears started to fall. "You didn't come and you didn't call. You didn't even write. I thought…" At that moment, both of us was overcome with three years-worth of sadness and longing. With nothin' but a thin piece of glass between us, we touched each other's hand and cried and cried. Between choking sobs, I told her how much I always loved her and tried to explain how Hank wouldn't let me contact her—even tore up my letters. Caught me tryin' to phone the prison and beat me somethin' terrible. Through her tears, she said she understood and she was so sorry for doubting my love. Imagine that! Amy apologized to *me*. My heart sat in a puddle right there on the cold, gray table. I promised her I'd get her out of that dreadful place and we'd be together again. I told her how Sergeant Travers and Edith was tryin' to help us, and how I got a raise at work but Hank didn't know about it.

"Mama, where's Jodie? Where's my baby girl?" she finally asked. I knew it was comin' but still I weren't prepared to answer. How could I tell her what Jodie was goin' through? How could I justify lettin' Hank treat her like a worthless piece of rubbish?

"Listen, Amy, she's gonna be okay. I'm workin' on a plan."

"What do you mean 'gonna'? What has he done to her? Where is she? Tell me!" Now, her eyes lookin' wild, she dropped her hand to the table forceful, and I started feelin' afraid again. Would she ever be able to forgive me for lettin' our Jodie suffer?

Real quiet, I explained, "Jodie's been livin' with us, but you can't tell the sergeant." With one hand, I covered the receiver and turned to see if Sergeant Travers could hear me. He just nodded and smiled as if to say "Yer doin' fine," so I continued. "If he knew about her livin' with us, he'd have her taken away and we might never see her again."

"What do you mean? Why? Why would she be taken away? What has Daddy been doin' to her?" Her voice was getting louder, and she started lookin' around to make sure nobody heard her. "Tell me, Mama," she said, her eyes boring into mine like she wanted to kill me.

"Oh, Amy, I'm so sorry," I said, tryin' to figure a way to tell her so she wouldn't go completely crazy. I was shakin' and breathin' hard. Then, I started talkin' real fast so she couldn't interrupt me. "She's okay, but she ain't been goin' to school or nothin'. She's six years old now and she looks just like you did at that age. She don't talk much, but I tell her about her mama all the time. I know she remembers you, and she knows you love her, and you want to be with her. I told Jodie I got a plan, and she and me will be leavin' Hank soon. I'll get you a good lawyer and get you outta prison so we can be toge—"

Well, the fast talkin' didn't work 'cause Amy stopped me in the middle of my blathering, and—with a look of horror contortin' that pretty face—she growled in a voice I didn't recognize.

"What the hell has Daddy done to my baby?"

"It's gonna be okay. She's gonna be okay. I promise." As I grabbed my cane and stood to leave, Sergeant Travers approached and held my elbow to steady me.

"Is everything okay here?" he asked.

"Yes, everything's fine. I just need to leave now," I answered.

"No, you can't leave until you tell me!" She was becoming hysterical, which drew the attention of a matron. I had to get outta there. I had put the phone down, 'cause I couldn't bear to hear my baby rantin' so crazy-like. I had to leave before she got the truth outta me. It broke my heart to see her so upset, but I was sure she'd be even more upset if she knew how her precious little girl was bein' treated.

Now two matrons was leading her away. As she struggled to release their clutch she was shoutin' at me over her shoulder like a madwoman. I hoped she wouldn't get in trouble for bein' disruptive, but I vowed she'd never know the truth about Jodie. It would destroy her. As Sergeant Travers led me back to the waiting bench, I kept tryin' to reassure Amy, with my eyes, that everything would be okay. I threw kisses and waved "good-bye" to my pitiful girl. I hated to see her in such pain but it was for the best. I had to believe once I got us outta that house—me and Jodie—everything would be okay, and Amy wouldn't ever have to know how bad it had been.

"What happened?" the sergeant asked when we finally reached his truck. "It seemed like you two were getting along so well. What set her off like that?"

I was still shakin' and I tried to get ahold of my nerves. "I don't know," I lied. "We was talkin' about her daddy and she just lost it. She remembers how bad he always treated us. I guess the memories just come floodin' back and she couldn't take it."

"I knew it must be bad for *you* living with Hank, but that poor girl has been seriously traumatized."

"He used to beat her somethin' awful, never even wanted her from the get-go, but I was already pregnant when Henry... To tell you the truth, sergeant, she's better off in prison."

"Not if I have anything to do about it. Stella, it's time to get you out of that house before Hank kills you."

"I know, but I can't leave, not till I have enough money saved to get far away and start fresh. I was thinkin' maybe I could go to one of them shelters till I get on my feet."

"That's a good idea," he said. "Edith and I can help." He started to turn the key in the ignition, then paused to touch my shoulder and look me straight in my eyes like my daddy used to when he had somethin' important to tell me. "Stella," he said, "You need to pack a bag and hide it some place where Hank won't find it. You need to be ready when the time is right to escape. I know a place you can go. It's called Agape Shelter and it isn't far from the café. You'd still be able to work there."

"I been readin' about that place... found a pamphlet at the café... memorized the hotline number, too," I said.

"That's good." he said, like he was proud of me. "That's real good."

"But Hank knows where I work. What if he shows up at the café?"

"Listen, Stella. I think Hank's about to get himself arrested."

"Arrested? How? When?"

"Saturday morning. We have an operation set up to catch him and the dirt-bags he's been buying from." I started to feel panicky when he told me that. It was all movin' too fast. I hadn't even called the shelter yet. I hadn't figured how to get Jodie unstrapped from that chain. I didn't have enough money saved yet. I started feelin' doubts about everything. Maybe it wasn't so bad livin' with Hank. Maybe I wasn't a "battered wife." Maybe I needed to try harder to keep Hank happy. But then I remembered my precious grand-daughter. No! I couldn't let one more week pass with her livin' in that dark room and bein' chained to a bed with only enough food to keep a bug alive. The sergeant was right. It was time to act.

"I'll call the shelter, Stella," he said. "I know the staff there and they know me. I'll ask them to prepare a bed for you. You'll be able to stay up to three months and it costs nothing. You'll be able to save your paychecks until you can afford a place of your own. If something should go wrong Saturday morning I want to make sure you're out of that house, okay?"

"Okay," I said, mindlessly. I was kinda numb and not sure what I was agreeing to.

"When you get home tonight, after Hank goes to sleep, I want you to pack a bag and hide it. Be sure to take any important papers—like your birth certificate and Amy's, your social security card, stuff like that—and medi-cines. If you have any cash, make sure you take it with you."

"Okay." There it was again. I just kept sayin' "okay" but I was thinkin', How am I gonna do this? If Hank catches me, he'll kill me for sure. Then there won't be nobody to protect Jodie. He'll kill her, too. Amy will never forgive me if I let Hank kill Jodie. I'll never forgive myself.

When I got back to the café, my head was swimmin'. I had two days to get ready... two days to get Jodie ready. What if they take her away from me because of how she looks? I got to make sure she gets a bath and her hair washed. I got to sneak more food to her somehow. I got to make sure she has somethin' decent to wear—not that raggedy-lookin' dress. How am I gonna do all that before Saturday without Hank noticin'?

When Sergeant Travers—he told me to call him Mike, but it don't seem right, somehow—when Sergeant Travers dropped me at the café, Edith was in the kitchen. I heard her talkin' to Louie. I went straight to her office and closed the door so she wouldn't start askin' a lot of questions. I had to do some thinkin' first. What if I got her to pick me up Saturday? I could explain about Jodie and ask her not to tell the sergeant. She could drive us both to the shelter. I'd have to figure out the rest after we was safe.

Jodie

I ain't been feeling so good. I didn't hardly sleep last night. I don't feel like playing with my chicken-bone doll or looking at my picture book or anything. I couldn't eat this morning, just left my cereal for the mice to finish. Most mornings I can't wait for Stella to bring my cereal and I eat every drop. Lick the bowl, too.

My arms and legs been aching something awful and I'm real cold. Maybe I'm dying. Ha! That'll show Hank. Of course, if I die Stella will get all the beatings. I don't think she can take much more. Lately, I been wondering what it feels like to be dead. The preacher in the television box talks about a place called heaven where we go when we die. It sounds real nice and pretty, too. He says someday we'll be in heaven with Jesus... not Hank, of course. If Hank was in that heaven-place it wouldn't be nice at all. Maybe if I just go to sleep, I'll wake up in heaven with Jesus and Mama. I wish Mama would come for me. I wish Stella would come home. I wish somebody would hold me and sing to me. I need to cry some... maybe a lot. I best get started so I can finish before Hank gets home.

Edith

I thought I heard Stella return to the restaurant. She must have gone straight to my office. It seemed almost like she was trying to avoid me. I had spent the whole morning wondering how the visit with Amy was going. I prayed Amy wouldn't be too hard on her mother. The poor woman had been through so much already. When I saw that my office door was closed, I decided to leave her alone for a while. Maybe the visit had upset her and she needed some privacy to process everything. Three years is a long time to be separated from your child. I'm sure the reunion must have been an emotionally draining experience. I'd get the scoop from Mike later, anyway.

Finally, around two-thirty Stella came out, her face looking even more drawn than usual. I was in the dining room checking the place settings for dinner when she appeared at the entrance.

"Edith?" she called timidly. "Can I see you for a minute?"

"Of course, Stella. I didn't even hear you come back," I said. "Is everything okay?"

"Sure. I just need you to check the quarterly report." A few customers from the lunch crowd were lingering, but I knew Melinda could handle them. I followed Stella into the office and she closed the door behind us. I sensed this conversation wouldn't be about the quarterly report.

"How did it go at the prison?" I asked, trying to sound casual.

"It was fine... well, not exactly fine, but I need to ask a favor."

"Of course. What is it?" I motioned for her to sit in my desk chair. I pulled another chair up beside it and made a mental note to get Stella her own desk and computer soon.

"Sergeant Travers says I need to be ready to move out Saturday morning. He says the cops are plannin' to catch Hank buyin' drugs and arrest him. It's my chance to leave but I got no way."

"You can stay with me, Stella." I said.

"Oh, no, Ma'am. I mean, they's a shelter. The sergeant's gonna call and get me a room. It's just that I got no way of getting there and I was wonderin' if you could... well if you would maybe drive me." She looked so worried and anxious, I wondered if she had something else on her mind.

"Of course, I'll drive you. Is that all? Is there anything else I can do?" She seemed more agitated than relieved, and I felt like I needed to reassure her this was the right thing for her to do. "I know change is scary, Stella, but you can do this. You *need* to do this."

"I know. You're right. It's just that... if I tell you something—something real bad—will you promise not to tell Sergeant Travers?"

"Stella, what could be worse than Hank hitting you and degrading you every day? You can tell me anything. I'm your friend and you can trust me."

"You won't wanna be my friend when you hear this," she said. She stood and turned away from me toward the room's only window.

"Stella, what is it?" I asked, standing and placing my hands on her shoulders. "What are you trying to tell me? Is it about your visit with Amy?"

"Oh, Amy. I'm so sorry. I'm so sorry." Now she turned toward me, buried her face in my shoulder and wept. My heart ached for this woman who had been to hell and back. I'd do anything for her if she'd just let me. As suddenly as the waterworks had started, she stood erect and wiped her tears.

"I'm sorry, Edith. I didn't mean to... here's the quarterly report. I thought you might like to look it over." I took the papers from her and laid them back on the desk.

"Listen, Stella, if we're going to be friends, we have to be honest with each other. Friendship is based on trust."

"Yes, Ma'am. Trust. Okay. Hank goes out between nine and ten o'clock on Saturday mornings. Can you pick us up after he leaves?"

"Us?" I asked.

"Me and Jodie. That's what I need to tell you."

Feeling like I had been struck by lightning, I took a step backward. Then, working to hide my obvious shock, I asked as calmly as I could manage, "Jodie will be with you?"

"Yes, but don't tell the sergeant, please!"

"But why? He'll be thrilled. He has been trying to locate her."

"You said friendship is about trust, right?"

"Yes, absolutely."

"He can't know nothin' about Jodie right now. I need for you to trust *me* on that. You can't tell nobody she's been livin' with us. So, can you pick us up and carry us to the shelter?"

"Yes, I'll be there." I had so many questions. I hated keeping secrets from Mike, but I couldn't risk Stella changing her mind about leaving Hank. I would get my answers later—once Stella and her granddaughter were safe.

"Thank you. I owe you."

"You don't owe me anything, Stella. I'm glad to help."

Chapter 13

Stella

My plan was to get Jodie all cleaned up and dressed early so we'd be ready and waitin' when Edith come. I got up before Hank and crept out of the bedroom as quiet as a mouse—which ain't easy with this here cane. On Saturdays, Hank don't usually think about nothin' but gettin' them drugs. I was countin' on him not checkin' on Jodie before he went out. Friday mornin' I managed to pack us a bag—like Mike said to—and hid it in the utility room beside the water heater. I covered it up with dirty clothes. We never did have a dryer, so they's plenty of room in the corner. You can bet I got my money-stash from under the kitchen sink, too.

The night before, Hank nearly caught me searchin' in his dresser drawers for the key to Jodie's strap. I made up a story about putting his clean underwear away. He cussed at me but he didn't hit me. I was thinkin' to myself, *Maybe I won't never get hit by Hank again after today,* but I sure was scared somethin' would go wrong. If our plan didn't work and Hank come back, the beatings would be worse than ever.

I never did find that key, but I got a razor blade from the bathroom and hid it beside the water heater wrapped in a towel. As soon as Hank left, I'd use it to cut through the strap on Jodie's leg. I'd have to work fast before Edith come. I didn't want her to see how we lived in this here shack of a place with the peeling paint, messed up floor boards, and second-hand furniture. Lord knows I tried to keep it clean, but the landlord didn't do nothin' to maintain it and Hank sure didn't help none. It was a roof over our heads but that's about it. I felt ashamed for Edith to see it and to see Jodie but I needed her help. Who else could I ask? What I weren't countin' on was her bringing a social worker with her.

Well, they musta been waitin' and watchin' for Hank to leave because no sooner did I hear his truck pull away and there's a knock at the door. I panicked. I couldn't let Edith see Jodie chained to the bed. Wouldn't you know Hank got up early. I didn't even have time to get Jodie washed up and changed outta that nasty dress. I tried to stall. I called through the door that I weren't dressed yet.

"Hurry, Stella! We might not have much time!" Edith hollered back. Then I could hear her talkin' to somebody, and I knowed she weren't alone. What if she brought the cops? No. She wouldn't do that. I told her I'd be right out. Then I quick got the razor blade and towel and went to Jodie's room. She was still sleepin' which weren't like her. She hadn't even touched her cereal, and she was curled up in a ball lookin' real peaked. I tried to be gentle on her leg but she moaned like I was hurtin' her. I wrapped the towel around her ankle for padding and started cuttin' through the strap. That's when she screamed. In that dark room—Hank never would let me put a light bulb in the socket—I thought I musta cut Jodie. I didn't see how, as careful as I was bein'. I went to the window and pulled the blanket down so I could see better. In come the bright sunlight. Jodie ain't used to light and she hollered again. Well, that's when Edith and the other woman come burstin' through the door, thinkin' I don't know what. They found me leanin' over Jodie with a razor blade and her lookin' like one of them prison camp Jews after the world war. I ain't never seen such shock and horror on anybody's face as I saw on that other woman's face.

"What in the name of God?" she asked through her hands that was coverin' her mouth. She stood there like she couldn't move, lookin' plum horrified. Then she started firing questions—one after the other—not waitin' for me to explain. "What *is* this? What's going on here? Is that a child? What's that smell? What have you done to her? Oh, my dear Lord!" Her voice kept getting louder and Jodie was lookin' real scared. She was all curled up in a ball, hidin' her eyes and whining like a hurt puppy. I couldn't figure what to do next. So, I just started cuttin' that strap, frantic-like.

"You got to help me. I got to get her loose," I pleaded. I was down on my knees tryin' like everything to cut through the leather and now Jodie was cryin' out and pullin' away because of them strangers.

"Move away from the child now!" the woman screamed as she pulled on my arm. "Edith, call an ambulance… and the police."

That's when I realized she thought Jodie was pullin' away from me, that I was tryin' to hurt her. Everything was happening so fast. I fell backwards and the razor blade clanked on the floor beside me. The woman was tryin' to settle Jodie but Jodie wouldn't let her touch her. She was huddled in the corner as far as the chain would allow. She covered her eyes—which weren't used to the light—and she looked so scared. I wanted to take her in my arms and comfort her but the woman wouldn't let me near my own grandchild. At that moment, I knowed my Jodie was gonna' be taken away from me and I might never see her again. She needed me. She didn't have nobody else and she needed me.

Then Edith come back in the room. "Paramedics are on their way," she said. She covered Jodie with the blanket from the window and now my poor, scared baby girl looked no bigger than a newborn all curled up into a ball like that with her eyes shut tight and her hands coverin' her ears. That's when memories of Henry come floodin' back and I started crying hysterically and sayin' I don't know what. The other woman went outside to meet the ambulance, and Edith sat beside me on the floor with her arms around my shoulders. She was tryin' to get me calmed down. I felt like I was losin' my mind. All I wanted was to get Jodie and me to a safe place and now this.

"Oh, Stella," Edith said. "You should have told me. I could've helped." She seemed so sad and she was crying, too. Jodie was quiet now and we just sat there rockin' and cryin' together until we heard the sirens wailing. I collapsed in Edith's arms and stayed there while the paramedics cut Jodie loose and loaded her on a gurney. I couldn't watch. I weren't allowed near her, anyway. Now she didn't make a sound and I wondered if she were dead. Maybe they give her a shot to calm her. I don't know. My face was buried in Edith's shoulder and I was wonderin' if I'd ever see my Jodie again.

"Come on, Stella. Let's get you out of here," Edith said as she helped me to my feet. I musta told her where my bag was because she handed it to me once I settled in the passenger seat of her car. I guess the other woman went with Jodie in the ambulance. All I could think about was if I'd ever see Jodie again, and how would I explain to Amy what happened to her daughter. How would I explain to Edith what she and the other woman saw in that room?

Edith

I wanted to take Stella to my apartment, but, honestly, I was afraid I'd get charged with harboring a criminal. I was already in trouble for not calling the cops as Ms. Cartwright had instructed me. I decided I had better get Stella to the shelter. I would call Mike as soon as I got her settled.

Oh, Stella, why couldn't you have trusted me enough to tell me everything? Who knows how long the child has been neglected and abused. I'd never seen or imagined anything like that disgusting scene before. It was shocking... and the smell. My God! The smell!

What kind of monster could chain an innocent child to a bed? Jodie was six years old but she was the size of a three-year-old. She looked like a trapped wild animal that had long ago given up hope of ever being set free. The tiny room with no lights resembled a tomb. I guessed the tattered brown blanket on the floor had covered the room's only window. The solitary piece of furniture was an old, rusty iron bed that stood against the far wall. It was covered with a filthy mattress—no sheets or blankets—and that poor child was chained to the foot-railing by a strap around her ankle. Next to the bed sat a pot, reeking of urine and feces. Shock doesn't begin to describe my reaction. I prayed that Hank Leonard had been caught that morning and hauled off to jail where he would rot in a cell for the rest of his life. I wanted him to suffer for what he had done to Jodie and Stella—and Amy, too.

Without Ms. Cartwright to direct me to the shelter, I had to call. Mike had said it wasn't far from my restaurant but I didn't know the exact location. I just knew I had to get Stella away from the dreadful hovel of a house filled with memories that I couldn't imagine in my worst nightmare. Judging from the social worker's reaction, I suspected Stella would be charged as an accessory to child abuse--if not worse--but we would cross that bridge later.

As I phoned the shelter, Stella sat motionless in the passenger seat, slumped over her duffel bag. She was holding on to it like it was her singular lifeline. No longer crying, she stared at the floor, looking so despondent that I wondered if she might become suicidal. It frightened me.

Once we got underway, I tried to engage Stella in conversation about the potential resources at Agape House and how I was going to hire a good lawyer for her, but she only shook her head for "no" or nodded for "yes." She continued to stare at the floor as if frozen in that near-fetal position. As we pulled into the 7-Eleven parking lot, where we were instructed to meet a worker from the shelter, Stella appeared to be in a hypnotic state.

Soon, I spotted the green Ford Focus that had been described to me over the phone. Reluctant to turn her over to a stranger, I helped Stella alight from my car and walk, unsteadily, toward the young woman who approached us. She said her name was Jessica, and that she was a regular volunteer at Agape House. I introduced myself and Stella, but Stella remained silent, clutching that ragged duffel bag. You would've thought it was a designer handbag from Prada. Together, Jessica and I transferred Stella to the front passenger seat of the Ford, and wedged her cane in beside her. "Is the shelter nice?" I asked Jessica. "I mean, will she be comfortable? I don't think she should be left alone. I think she might be in shock." Suddenly, I realized I wasn't giving Jessica a chance to respond, but I was so worried about Stella. I was desperate for reassurance.

"Don't worry, Edith, we'll take good care of her. The shelter is a lovely Cape Cod-style house, and the rooms are pleasant. The staff is wonderful, too. She'll be quite comfortable and safe, I promise." She knew exactly what I needed to hear.

"Thank you," I said, finally relaxing a bit. "May I have a minute?" I asked, nodding toward Stella.

"Of course. Take all the time you need."

"Stella," I said, kneeling and placing my hand gently on her knee. "Can you hear me?" Finally, she looked up. When her vacant eyes met mine, I wondered if she needed medical attention.

"Jodie. Where's Jodie?" she asked as she glanced about the vehicle like she was seeing it for the first time.

"Jodie has gone to the hospital. She'll receive good care there."

"She needs me. She'll be scared and she needs me."

"You can visit her after a while. I'll take you to the hospital as soon as possible, okay?"

"She needs me now. I'm all she's got."

"Right now, she needs to get well and strong, and you must get settled in your new home. Do you know where you are going?" I asked.

"Shelter," she answered weakly.

"That's right, you're going to the Agape House, and you'll be safe now."

"Safe," she repeated in her robot-like trance. She appeared so tired and beaten.

"Why don't you take a nice long nap this afternoon?" I suggested.

"Nap," she repeated, faintly. Reluctantly, I stood, closed the door and watched as Jessica drove away.

As soon as I returned to my car, I called Mike. I was anxious to hear how the raid went and whether Hank had been arrested. If anything went wrong and Hank were still at-large, both Stella's and Jodie's lives could be in worse danger than ever.

"Edith, we got him. We got the whole damn ring!" Mike exclaimed without as much as a "hello." He sounded more excited than a sixteen-year-old who just passed his driving test. I had never heard him swear before. He was so fired up, I felt reluctant to tell him what Ms. Cartwright and I had discovered at Hank's house. It would bring him down for sure.

"Oh, Mike! That's wonderful news! So, Hank is in jail?"

"He sure is! Of course, who knows how long he'll stay there, but for now Stella is safe."

"After what I saw this morning, I don't think we're going to have to worry about Hank Leonard getting out of prison for a very long time. Now if we can just keep Stella from going to prison…"

"Why? What do you mean?"

"Mike, you're not going to believe—listen, can you come to the café for dinner tonight?"

"You bet. I can't wait to grab you and plant a huge celebration kiss on your sexy lips. But it sounds like you have something on your mind, Edith. Did you run into some trouble about the shelter?"

"No, Stella's on her way, but I've got to get to the café for the lunch shift. I'll see you tonight and tell you everything."

"Okay. I'm just returning to the station to write my report. I'll see you around six. Edith, are you all right?"

"I'm fine, Mike. I'll see you later. Oh, and congratulations again. Bye."

Mike

I was flying high after that drug bust. What a coup for the captain and for our whole precinct. It turns out that, in the process of staking out a small-time junkie like Hank Leonard, we uncovered a major operation with possible connections throughout the entire country. The narcotics division is confident it's only a matter of time before the FBI locates Vasquez. In the meantime, we caught some of his major players who will squeal like stuck pigs when they're faced with a lifetime in prison. High school kids, my eye! Who would have thought a small town like ours was connected to an international drug ring? Hank didn't have a clue. That's for sure. All he cared about was getting his next fix. This is exactly the break I needed to convince Captain Howard to reopen Amy's case.

I'm a little worried about what went down with Stella this morning. Edith sounded like she was hiding something. At least Stella is out of that wretched place and in the shelter for now. It's doubtful Hank has the means to raise bail but you never know. In the meantime, he'll have all he can handle with detox. I'll get the low-down from Edith tonight.

Jodie

I woke up in this bright room. Don't know how long I been sleeping. There's something stuck to my hand, and nice ladies keep asking me questions and calling me Sweetie. How do they know the name I gave myself? I ain't talked to nobody. I can't hardly open my eyes because the light hurts 'em real bad. Where's Stella? Why doesn't she come? I'm so sleepy and my legs hurt, especially when the ladies rub on them.

I think this might be General Hospital like on the television box. It's a place where sick people go and has doctors and nurses taking care of them. I hear the same noises like on General Hospital. Maybe the nice ladies are nurses. How did I get here? Where's Stella?

I feel so warm and safe in this bed… not like my bed that's cold and smells bad. This bed has warm covers and feels soft. Guess that's why I can't stay awake. So sleepy…

Chapter 14

Edith

I called the shelter to check on Stella, but they wouldn't let me talk to her. The woman who answered the phone said it was for her safety and the safety of the other residents.

"But I'm her friend... and her boss," I explained. "I just want to know how she's doing."

"Is this Edith?" the woman asked.

"Yes. Edith Bowman. I'm the one who turned Stella over to Jessica."

"Hi, Edith. I'm Wendy. I manage the shelter. I can assure you Stella is fine. She slept right through lunch, but I had the cook make her a sandwich and took it to her myself."

"Oh, good. I was worried about her. In fact, I wanted to alert you that I think Stella could be in danger of taking her life. She was in a bad way when I left her."

"That's possible. Many women are potentially suicidal upon arrival. We keep a close watch on them until we're sure of their mental stability."

"That's a relief. Listen, would it be possible for me to visit Stella? I mean, I understand you must be careful, but..."

"Yes, but you'll need to put in a request with social services. I can do that for you, if you like. As soon as you're cleared to visit, they'll arrange for a designated police officer to meet you somewhere and drive you here."

"Okay. I appreciate your help, Wendy. Oh, one more thing. Stella works at my restaurant and she doesn't have transportation. She'll need a few days off, of course, but once she starts back…"

"Stella won't be able to leave Agape House until her case worker can be sure of her safety."

"Oh, her husband—her abuser—is in jail. He got arrested. Just this morning."

"That's good, but jail time is never a guarantee. We've seen too many cases where the abuser gets out on bail or on a technicality and re-offends, usually more violently than ever."

"Really? That's terrible!"

"Anyway," Wendy continued, "I'll try to get you cleared for a visit tomorrow afternoon. Someone from social services will call you." I thanked her for her help and for taking care of Stella. I longed to wrap my arms around Stella and tell her everything was going to be okay. At the same time, I appreciated the diligence with which she was being protected.

Mike

I could hardly wait to see Edith and tell her about the stakeout. I could hardly wait to see Edith, period. I seemed to be thinking about her around the clock. As soon as I got off work, I made a beeline for the café.

Edith was mingling with the customers, as usual, moving from one table to another with her back to the entrance. When she turned around and spotted me her face lit up. *That's what a man likes to see when he enters a room,* I thought. I wanted to grab her and plant a big, wet smooch on those sensual lips, but I'd never risk embarrassing her in front of her employees and customers.

"Good evening, Sergeant Travers," she said as she approached me, speaking louder than necessary. The initial smile had disappeared and was replaced by her all-business demeanor as she motioned toward the rear of the restaurant. "Can you come to my office for a minute?"

"Sure. What's up?" Edith led me behind the counter, past the kitchen, and into her office. She closed the door behind us. Then, without warning, she pinned me against the wall, reached behind my neck, and pulled my lips down to hers. Electricity surged through my body as we engaged in a passionate kiss accompanied by so much osculating I nearly forgot I was a gentleman.

"I've been waiting all day for that," Edith said breathlessly when we finally came up for air.

"I don't usually have dessert before dinner," I whispered, planting butterfly kisses on her ears and neck, "but I could be convinced to change my usual habits."

"To be continued tomorrow night," she said seductively, grabbing my hand and leading me to a chair. "Now tell me everything."

"Everything? Oh. You mean about this morning. Holy smokes, Edith! Give a man a chance to catch his breath!"

"Okay, but only a minute. Do you want the special?" She walked to the door and opened it.

"I've lost my appetite... for food, that is," I said, trying to slow my breathing. She laughed and called toward the kitchen.

"Louie, roast chicken for the sergeant, please. He'll eat in my office."

"You got it, boss," Louie answered. Then Edith pulled her chair close to mine and sat facing me.

"I like a take-charge woman," I said, playfully, hoping my innuendo might prolong the sexual tension between us. But Edith had already switched gears.

"Okay, spill it, Mike. Tell me how the raid went down." As I described the events leading up to Hank's arrest, I was all too aware that our knees were touching. Edith hung on every word.

"How exciting! I can't believe such a major operation took place right here in our little town in broad daylight."

"That's how Vasquez kept it under the radar for so long. No one expected him to set up here. Remember that furniture factory down by the railroad crossing that went under during the recession?"

"Sure. A lot of people in this town lost their jobs."

"Well, it turns out one of Vasquez's flunkies bought it for storing 'furniture' imported from China. It was the perfect cover. The furniture crates arrived in Wilmington by ship and were transferred to trucks that took them across the state to a warehouse on the property right here. This afternoon one of the junior members of the organization—a guy we nabbed earlier—spilled his guts and tipped off the detectives to that warehouse. It didn't take Captain Howard long to get a search warrant. Can you guess what the SWAT team found in half of those crates?"

"Drugs, of course. Oh, Mike! What a lucky break. Here comes Louie with your dinner." Edith stood and cleared a place on her desk for me to eat. "I need to check the register," she said, "but I'll be back in a minute. Can I bring you something to drink?"

"Sure. A Coke would be great." When Edith returned a few minutes later, I had nearly finished Louie's generous helpings of roasted chicken and dressing smothered in gravy, sautéed green beans, and homemade rolls that melted in my mouth. Dessert was out of the question. I leaned against the back of the chair, feeling like I needed to loosen my belt. "That French restaurant was good," I noted, "but nothing beats Louie's comfort food."

"I'm blessed to have found him, that's for sure," she agreed. She handed me a Coke with lots of crushed ice—just the way I like it.

"Thanks. Now it's your turn. You said you found something interesting at Stella's place."

"Interesting doesn't begin to cover it," she said. She proceeded to tell me about discovering Jodie's whereabouts. As she described the child's physical state and the conditions in which she was living, I thought I might lose my dinner. I couldn't believe what I was hearing. How could Stella keep it a secret all these years? How could anyone treat an innocent child so hideously? Why didn't she report Hank to the authorities? So many questions were swirling in my head. Stella could have gotten Jodie out of that situation long ago. The child could have been under Child Protective Services while her mother was in prison. CPS would have found her a foster family, and Hank would have been arrested much sooner. But as Edith continued to communicate the events of the morning, I recalled my training in Battered Woman Syndrome. I began to understand how Stella must have felt helpless and afraid.

"Do you think Jodie will be all right?" I asked.

"She looked pretty bad, but I hope so. I promised Stella I'd visit her in the hospital soon and report back to her. Do you think Stella will be charged with child abuse?"

"It's probable. Child neglect, at least," I answered.

"But you and I both know she loves that child."

"We know nothing of the sort. Stella never even mentioned Jodie was in the house."

"You're right, but... oh, Mike! Stella has been through so much, and now she has a chance to start over—to have a good life. We must help her somehow."

"You've already helped her, Edith. You've gotten her out of that horrible environment and into a safe house. That's a good start."

"I guess so. I just wish I could do more. Well, Sergeant Sexy," she continued as she rose to leave, "I have a large party arriving at seven. So, I need to get back to the dining room. Did you have enough to eat?"

"Not so fast. Back up. Sergeant what?" I teased, as I grabbed her hand

and pulled her to me.

"You heard me. My, my! Aren't we needy."

"You have no idea," I declared, embracing and kissing her hungrily. With reluctance, we parted, but not before Edith nibbled my ear and whispered, "I'll see you in the morning, Mike." A cold shower would be in order before I could settle into an evening of studying for the lieutenant's exam.

Edith

Monday afternoon, I was allowed to visit Stella. When I reached her room, she was sitting on the edge of the bed, halfheartedly brushing her hair. I had never seen her hair relaxed around her face like that. She always had it pulled back in a bun for work. Even with the abundance of gray, stringy streaks, the loose tresses took years off her face. She looked more rested and alert than when I had left her the day before.

"Hi, Stella. How are you feeling?"

"Okay," she answered without raising her head.

"I brought you something to eat."

"I ain't—I'm not—hungry."

"I'll just set it here on the night stand, and you can eat it whenever you feel hungry." I sat on the bed beside her, gently removed the brush from her hand, and began brushing her hair. "Do you feel like talking?" I asked.

"Don't know what good it'll do."

"Stella, I know you wouldn't hurt your granddaughter. I know you were trying to help her."

"Then why did you bring that woman?"

"It's policy, Stella. The shelter always sends a social worker."

"I shoulda let CPS take her long ago. I was scared I'd never see her again... that Amy'd never see her again. I tried to protect her from Hank. I tried to take care of her but he wouldn't let me. I failed! I failed everybody! I ain't fit to be Amy's mama and I ain't fit to be Jodie's grandmama. I *ain't* nobody and now I *got* nobody," she cried. She turned toward me and fell into my arms like a ragdoll.

I felt helpless as she sobbed miserably. I didn't know how to comfort this despairing woman because her situation did, indeed, seem hopeless. She and I both realized how yesterday morning's scene appeared to Ms. Cartwright, and we knew what the woman would be reporting to Child Protective Services. I held Stella and rocked her as she spent her tears. I prayed that God would give me some words to comfort her, to help her envision a life worth living. Then it came to me. Out of nowhere, I started singing a hymn that I had probably sung a thousand times before. I had grown up in the church and learned countless hymns through the years. It never ceased to amaze me how those hymn writers of long ago managed to capture the deep longings of every human heart through the ages. I was also amazed at how the words would resurface just when I needed them—when I didn't even realize I had committed them to memory. As I rocked Stella gently and stroked her hair, I began to sing:

What a friend we have in Jesus, all our sins and griefs to bear.
What a privilege to carry everything to God in prayer!
Oh, what peace we often forfeit. Oh, what needless pain we bear,
All because we do not carry everything to God in prayer!

There were more verses, but I couldn't remember them. I just kept singing the same verse over and over, swaying back and forth with Stella wrapped in my firm embrace, trying to offer comfort. Soon, her muscles began to relax. As her breathing slowed, she raised her head and wiped her tears. "Edith?" she asked. "Will you help me pray?"

"Of course, I will," I said. I held her hands in mine and we bowed our heads. I uttered a very simple prayer, one line at a time, that she could repeat after me. I was reminded of a period in my life—some seven years earlier—when I had felt so grief-stricken I couldn't pray. I remembered how much it meant to have others pray for me and with me.

When we finished, Stella said, "I think I can eat some of that sandwich now."

"Good. That's good. Here. Sit back and I'll put the plate on your lap." I fluffed the pillows so she could sit erect and placed the sandwich in front of her. I was hesitant to leave until I felt confident she would be okay. I walked to the window. This room—located at the rear of the house—lacked the dormers that adorned the front. The double window let in plenty of natural light. The pretty curtains were translucent and billowy and framed a tree-filled backyard. *Such a pleasant room*, I thought as I glanced around at the homey touches. On the wall above the nightstand hung a picture of an adoring mother embracing her young child. Along with a vase of silk flowers, a basket of toiletries had been placed on the dresser. Whoever decorated this home-away-from-home understood the importance of comforting surroundings for women and children who have been living with constant worry and fear.

"Stella," I said, noticing she had eaten half the sandwich. "I need to get back to the café, but I'll check on you again soon. Will you be okay?"

"Yes, Ma'am. Yes, Edith. I'm fine, and I'm so beholden to you. You're a good friend. I thank you for helpin' me like you have."

"That's what friends do. They help each other. Now, don't forget to go to dinner. You have to keep up your strength for Jodie."

"Edith, you've done so much already. I hate to ask, but…"

"What is it? You know I'll do whatever I can."

"Well, could you… could you go see Jodie at the hospital? I need to know how she's doin'. I know she must be scared. I think she might be gettin' real sick, too. I'm worried about her."

"Of course. I'll go tomorrow. I was planning to check on her anyway. Since she doesn't know me, she probably won't talk to me but… Does she talk, Stella?"

"Not much. She ain't really talked since Hank chained her to that bed three years ago. He'd beat both of us if he ever caught me talkin' to her."

"I'm so sorry." My heart ached for her and for that poor defenseless child.

"Anyway, I thought she didn't remember how, but one day I was tellin' her about Amy and she said, 'Mama'. Oh Jodie! What have I done?"

"Don't blame yourself, Stella. You did what you thought you had to—to survive. Hank is in jail, and now you need to focus on the future—yours and Jodie's and Amy's, too."

"Hank got arrested? Hank's in jail?"

"Yes. I thought you knew but, of course, you didn't. How could you? You're safe now, Stella."

"Safe," she repeated. She took a deep breath, sighed, and closed her eyes. "We're safe, Jodie," she whispered.

I sat beside her on the bed and took her hands in mine. "You sleep well tonight, and I'll see you again after I visit Jodie."

"I can't remember the last time I slept the whole night through, but I reckon I will tonight." I gave her a hug and started to leave when she remembered something. "Edith, there's a Teddy bear in my bag."

"Yes, I saw it in your duffle bag."

"It's Jodie's. Amy give it to her for her third birthday but Hank wouldn't let her keep it. Threw it in the trash. But I dug it out and hid it. Will you take it to her? I think Jessica put my things in that drawer over there."

"Of course, I will." I retrieved the stuffed bear, gave Stella a hug, and beat a hasty retreat down the stairs and out the door, carrying that bear in my arms like it was the cherished baby I lost all those years before. I climbed in the police car, where I sat hugging the soft bear to my chest and crying for all the Jodie's and all the Stella's in the world who wonder, every day, when someone will rescue them. The kind police woman didn't say a word. She just laid a hand tenderly on my shoulder and let me empty my overflowing heart.

Stella

I think I finally got a real friend. I don't know why Edith cares about me but she seems real genuine. I think I can trust her. I should've trusted her earlier. Maybe we coulda got Jodie outta that awful room sooner. I'm worried she's real sick. I didn't notice how bad she looked till the light come in through that window. Once I thought us bein' together was the most important thing but now I know—even if I never see her again—the most important thing is for her to get better and have a good life. I just hope it ain't too late. *Oh Jodie! Can you ever forgive me? I loved you from the day you was born... but maybe I been selfish.*

When I first come here to the shelter, I hardly knew where I was or how I got here. Some woman named Jessica brought me and put me in this here room. She made me strip down to my underwear so she could take pictures of my bruises and scars. I didn't feel embarrassed at all. I didn't feel nothin', just kinda numb-like. When she was finished, she helped me under the covers of a real soft bed, and I guess I musta slept for a couple hours. When I woke up it was after lunchtime. That's when another nice woman named Wendy brought me a sandwich.

I'm feeling lots better today 'cause Edith came to see me. Edith said she'd go to the hospital to see how Jodie's doin'. I can't hardly wait for her to come back tomorrow and give me a report. If I get hauled off to jail it don't matter, just so Jodie's okay.

This here place seems nice and my room is real pretty. I feel like a queen livin' in a palace. After Edith left, I took the basket of soaps and lotions from the bureau and went down the hall to the bathroom. Well, you never saw such a tub! I ran it full of steamy hot water and poured in some of that purple bubble bath. It smelled like lilacs. Then, I got in and soaked and soaked till I couldn't feel or smell no traces of Hank on me. I washed my hair with some of that lilac shampoo and rinsed it real good. When I stepped outta the tub onto the soft blue bath mat and wrapped myself in one of them fluffy towels, I felt like a new woman. Besides my uniform, I owned only one pair of trousers. I pulled them on and put on a clean top. Then I pulled my hair back in a ponytail. When I looked in the mirror I wished I had some lipstick. I decided to ask Edith if she'd get me some.

I hadn't met nobody in the shelter except Jessica and Wendy. I worked up my nerve, grabbed my cane, and walked down the stairs. When I reached the bottom, by the front entrance, I heard talkin' in the front room off to my left. I was expectin' to see young women and children. I figured I'd be the oldest one here but there were three women, two of 'em about my age—maybe a little younger—settin' in the living room talkin'. They looked up when I come in and said "hi" to me.

"You must be Stella," the blonde one said. I needn't have worried about feelin' like an outsider because they was so friendly and introduced themselves right away. One was named Ruth. The blonde one was Samantha and the third one said her name was Julia. She was the one who let me and Jessica in the front door earlier, I think. Ruth's arm was in a sling and she had a bruise on her cheek. I didn't have to ask how she got hurt.

"Please join us," Ruth offered, pointing with her good arm to a worn, but comfortable-looking chair across from them.

"Okay, thanks," I answered, feeling kinda shy, but rememberin' this was my chance to make a new start. I sat down and rested my cane beside the chair. I tried to look at them other women's faces like I noticed Edith looked at people when she talked.

"How are you settling in?" Samantha asked.

"Just fine," I answered.

"Our room is across the hall from yours," Ruth said, motioning to Julia. Julia was quieter than the others and didn't smile.

"And I'm just down the hall across from the bathroom," added Samantha.

"Oh," I said, trying to look friendly.

"Don't worry, Stella. It gets easier after a few days," said Ruth.

"Okay, thanks." I was feeling like a fool, not knowin' what to say to these strangers.

"We were just talking about last night's group session," Ruth said. "You'll probably get started tomorrow. Each of us meets individually with a counselor once a week but we also have 'group' every evening at seven-thirty. I guess Wendy went over the schedule with you."

"No, not yet. Guess I fell asleep."

"Oh, well, she's the center director. She'll go over everything—probably tomorrow—and assign your chores."

"I thought it would be bigger, you know, more institutional-like," I said. "But it's like a real home."

"Yeah, we were surprised, too," Ruth said.

"I was expectin' kids, too."

"Oh, there are kids," laughed Samantha. "They live with their mothers in a separate building just over there." She pointed past me. "You'll see the young moms and their children at dinner."

"Speaking of which," Ruth said, glancing at her watch, "I'm on dinner duty, so I need to get going. Nice to meet you, Stella."

"You, too." Since Ruth was the most talkative one of the group, I worried it might get awkward after she left. I tried to think what to say. I never was much of a talker, and Hank didn't talk except to holler and cuss and give orders. Right then it occurred to me I had spent near twenty-five years tryin' not to say something that would make Hank mad.

Julia didn't seem to be much of a talker either. She had sad eyes—kinda like Amy's but brown.

Samantha saved the day. "Before you joined us, Stella, we were talking about last night's group session. Our counselor, Dr. Morgan, has been working with us on self-esteem. She says most battered women have low self-esteem which attracts domineering men. They see us as easy marks for their oppression."

"Yeah, like doormats." Julia said, bitterly. "I was such a fool to ever believe Brad when he said he loved me. But he was so charming while we were dating. He never laid a hand on me, and he was always bringing me gifts."

"Dr. Morgan called that 'grooming' remember? Brad was setting you up," Samantha said.

"How could I have missed the signs?" Julia asked. "How could I have been so stupid?"

"You weren't stupid, Julia. You thought you were in love. You thought he loved you. But real love is never abusive. Real love doesn't hurt."

"Now that I look back at both of my marriages," Samantha resumed, "I see what an easy target I was. With each husband, there were warning signs—you know—little alarm bells that went off in my head. But I ignored them because at first their behaviors were positive. Dr. Morgan said grooming works by starting with positive behaviors and words, then gradually mixing in subtle elements of abuse. It's very confusing because we want to give the benefit of the doubt to someone who showers us with the attention we crave. After a while the abusive behavior begins to feel normal. Let's see," Samantha continued, recalling more details from the session, 'desensitization'. That's what she called it. The abuser desensitizes his victim to the signs of abuse. I have a master's degree, Julia. I'm an intelligent woman with a good education and I ended up in *two* abusive relationships. So please stop calling yourself, 'stupid'. Dr. Morgan's point was that when we work on restoring our own self-worth, others will see us as worthy of respect and care."

"I thought I had everything a woman could ever wish for being married to a handsome, wealthy attorney," Samantha said. "By the time George made

District Attorney, we were living in a two-million-dollar mansion on River-side Drive. He bought me beautiful jewels and encouraged me to buy design-er clothes. We went to swank parties almost every weekend. I loved those parties because whenever we were in public George treated me like a queen. He seemed proud to show me off to his friends and colleagues. Now that I think about it, I didn't have any friends of my own. They were all George's friends. We had already agreed not to have children. I had planned to work and volunteer but he wouldn't let me. Once we were married he would act hurt and say I didn't appreciate all he provided for me."

"One night, after we came home from a party, he ripped off my Donna Karan original gown and stomped on it. He pushed me down on the floor and rubbed my face roughly against the fabric. Then he pulled the string of pearls from my neck and scattered them all over the bedroom floor. One-by-one he made me pick up each pearl and say 'thank you, darling.' Each time I tried to stand up, he pushed me back down with his foot and called me an 'ungrateful gold-digger' and worse."

At that point in her story I broke down. I couldn't believe what I was hearing. Mainly, I couldn't believe there was other women like me but from completely different walks of life. Smart, attractive—even rich—women was being hit, yelled at and humiliated every day just like me. I had been blamin' the drugs. Mostly, I blamed myself for Hank's anger and abuse, but them two women made me realize there was signs long before Henry died. I just chose to excuse them.

At that moment, Samantha and Julia seemed to recognize they had been ignoring me. They come and knelt beside my chair—one on each side of me. They put their hands on my shoulders and comforted me as only fellow victims can.

"It'll get better, Stella," Samantha said.

"Yeah, you've taken the first step—the hardest step," added Julia. "Now you just have to keep putting one foot in front of the other."

"We're all here to help each other," Samantha said, handing me a tissue. "Now, how about a game of Gin Rummy before dinner?"

I ain't never felt as cared for by anybody before except Mama and Edith. *Maybe I can make it*, I thought. *Maybe life ain't as hopeless as it seemed.*

Chapter 15

Edith

I awoke early Tuesday morning after a restless night. Not only did I find myself longing for Mike's strong embrace, but I couldn't stop thinking about Jodie. What that poor child has endured for three years—half of her young, pathetic life—is unimaginable. As I retrieved my newspaper from the corridor, I noticed the front-page article. It was about the drug bust. Although I was anxious to get to the hospital and find out how Jodie was doing, I switched on the local news. There it was again. I thought I might see Mike on TV but it was Captain Howard being interviewed. I felt relieved there was no mention of Stella or Jodie. It was only a matter of time before the reporters would catch wind of that juicy bit of news.

With the TV playing in the background, I dressed quickly. I wanted to do some shopping for Jodie today. She needed clothes and toys and books. She needed everything, and so did Stella.

As soon as Mike left the café and the breakfast crowd thinned out, I turned the restaurant over to Melinda for a couple of hours. I drove to Target and made a beeline for the toy department. There I selected a doll with long, blonde hair, a unicorn puzzle, some crayons and coloring books, a couple of picture books, and Play-Doh in four different colors. Next, I headed for the children's clothing department. I was having the time of my life and nearly forgot the actual time. I picked out two pretty, princess nightgowns—one in pink and one in yellow, also a pair of fuzzy slippers, plus underwear, socks, jeans and t-shirts—with sparkles, of course. I had to guess at the sizes. Because Jodie looked very small for her age, I went with fours. Shopping for Stella would have to wait. I needed to get to the hospital before I ran out of time. The lunch shift was always busy, and I knew the staff wouldn't be able to keep up without both Stella and me.

At the hospital, I checked in at the nurses' station to make sure it was okay for me to visit Jodie. Then, I stood outside Jodie's room with my packages, trying to bolster my courage to enter. I had been around lots of kids and always had a blast with my nieces, but this experience was different. Not knowing what to expect or how to act made me nervous. At the same time, I was excited to see how she would react to the gifts. According to Stella, the child had been chained to the bed for three years in that dingy, smelly room. Would she even know what Play-Doh was or how to play with a doll?

From inside the room I heard voices. Slowly I pushed open the door. Two nurses were helping the tiny sprite of a girl adjust to a walker. She could barely put one foot in front of the other, and the women were ever-so-gently encouraging every step. I observed that Jodie—who was wearing tiny, pink-rimmed sunglasses—appeared very frail and her skin was yellowish in color. I could easily have collapsed in tears at the sight but I knew I must hold myself together. A self-serving display of emotion would not help her in any way. I placed my bags on a chair and approached her slowly so as not to frighten her. She didn't seem to notice me until I was close enough to touch her—which I refrained from doing.

"Hi, Jodie," I said quietly. "I'm a friend of your grandma, Stella." I crouched down low to keep her from feeling threatened. "Wow. Look at you walking so well," I said.

"She has taken eight steps today, haven't you, Jodie?" one of the nurses remarked, cheerfully. "Later, we'll try for another eight, but let's get you back in bed now."

"May I stay for a while or does she need to rest?" I inquired.

"I'm sure she'd like some company," one of the nurses answered.

"And some conversation," added the other. "She's not talking yet, but a familiar face might encourage her to try." I decided not to divulge the fact that I was not exactly a familiar face to Jodie. I was afraid they might change their minds about letting me stay.

"See if you can get her to drink some of that juice. It has the electrolytes her body needs."

"Will do," I agreed as they lifted Jodie gently into one of two beds and tucked her under the covers. Acting surprisingly docile, she allowed them to complete their tasks without resistance.

"Yum, this juice looks good. How about a little drink?" I held the straw to her mouth. She took a sip, but most of it ran down her chin. "Oops! That didn't work too well, did it? Let's try it a different way." She allowed me to wipe her chin, and I offered the cup without the straw. That method seemed to work better. She took a few small sips.

"Jodie, my name is Edith. Your grandma, Stella, is a friend of mine."

"Stella?" she asked imploringly. Her husky voice both surprised and delighted me.

"Yes, Stella asked me to come, and she sends her love. She misses you, Jodie, and she'll come to see you soon. She sent you some presents. Would you like to see what I brought?"

She nodded her head slightly. *It's obvious she hasn't forgotten totally how to communicate,* I thought. I reached for the clothing bags first, and one-by-one began showing her the items. She seemed to especially like the fuzzy slippers which she rubbed against her cheeks. I watched with interest as she gathered everything close to her body and patted each item lovingly.

"Would you like to wear one of your new nightgowns?" I asked. She looked at me like she didn't understand what I was saying. I held up a nightgown and repeated the word, "Nightgown—would you like to wear it?" I placed it against her chest to show her how it would look on her.

"Nightgown," she repeated, patting it. I pulled off the price tag and began untying her hospital gown. As I removed it, I hoped she didn't hear me gasp when I saw the bruises that were hidden beneath it. Her chest, back, and upper arms were nearly covered with bruises—some faded and others inflicted recently. Her tiny body looked like it had been used as a punching bag. A foreign bulge on her left forearm betrayed that it had been broken at some point and had healed improperly. *The pain this child has endured is unspeakable,* I thought, as I struggled to hold back tears. I lowered the new garment gently over her head and helped her insert her tiny arms into the sleeves. When I pulled back the covers to adjust the gown, I noticed bruising on her legs and an ugly scar on her ankle, also significant bowing of those frail limbs. This poor child has been through hell! Dear Lord, I prayed silently, may her suffering end here and may she find enough love, joy, and peace—from this day forward—to erase the horrific memories. Amen.

To make space on her bed for the toys, I began to remove the other items, but Jodie gathered them close like she might never see them again.

"Okay, that's fine," I assured her and handed her the doll.

"Amy," she exclaimed, smiling for the first time. She remembered her mother. It must have been the long blonde hair that prompted her response.

"Yes, Amy," I agreed. She stroked the shiny hair and hugged the doll to her chest. I remembered the Teddy bear in my handbag. I pulled it out and handed it to her. "Mama," she said and grasped tightly both the doll and the bear. Then she lay back on the pillow, and, appearing exhausted, she closed her eyes. I decided the other toys could wait until my next visit. I sat for a few minutes watching her drift off to sleep as she clasped the doll and the Teddy bear, one in each arm. Hot tears began to burn my cheeks. Tears of anger mixed with overwhelming sadness flowed freely now, and I was glad Jodie couldn't see them. A nurse entered the room and—noticing my distress—tried to comfort me.

"She'll be okay," she said quietly, placing her hand on my shoulder. "It'll take time and lots of therapy, but she'll be okay. We caught the rickets in time, and with some proper nutrition…"

"Rickets?" I asked, wiping my nose.

"Yes, it's caused by a deficiency of vitamin D and calcium. It has weakened her bones but we should be able to reverse most of the damage."

"How long will she be hospitalized?" I asked, working to gain control of my emotions.

"At least a couple of weeks."

"Who will pay for her treatment?"

"She'll automatically receive Medicaid. I can promise she'll get the treatment she needs."

"After that, where will she go?"

"CPS has been notified and the social worker will be here this afternoon. She'll probably be fostered until a permanent home can be found."

"But she has a grandmother who loves her."

"I don't know anything about that. You'll have to talk to the social worker."

"What time will she… or he be here?"

"Oh, it'll be a woman. This child is terrified of men. I don't know what time she's coming."

"Just call me and I'll come right away. How long are you on duty, uh, Janine?" I asked, as I checked her name tag.

"My shift ends at seven."

"Please don't let the social worker leave without talking to me, okay, Janine? My name is Edith. Edith Bowman. Here's my phone number." I pulled a scrap of paper out of my purse and quickly scribbled my number on it.

"I'll do my best, Edith," she said.

"Thank you. It's really important."

Stella

After dinner last night, I had a meeting with the director. Her name is Wendy and she's real nice. She explained all the "house rules" to me and told me my chores. I have to keep my room clean and wash my own clothes. There's a laundry room with a washer and dryer and everything. We're supposed to sign a sheet telling what time we want to do our washin' so everybody gets a turn. This week my job is to vacuum the "common" rooms every other day—that's the rooms that everybody uses—like the living room, dining room, and "group" room. I have to work one meal every day, too, settin' the table, servin' the food, and clearin' the dishes. I asked for the dinner shift because I work at the café till four. I'm supposed to go to the group meeting every evening, too.

Wendy asked me if Hank knew where I work, and I told her it don't matter because he's in jail. She said I should keep track to make sure he don't get out and come lookin' for me. I told her I knew a cop who would warn me.

I couldn't hardly wait for Edith to come and tell me about visitin' Jodie. I had so many questions. Is Jodie scared? Did she ask for me? Is she eatin' okay? When can I go see her?

Dinner was pretty good—not like Louie's cookin' but good. Ruth showed me where the dishes and other stuff was so I'd be ready for my dinner shift startin' Monday.

I was nervous about the group meeting. I don't like to talk about feelings and personal stuff especially with strangers. I waited till right at seven-thirty to show up because I weren't sure if there was assigned seats. I didn't want to get off on the wrong foot by takin' somebody's chair. I worried about soundin' stupid, too. Them other women was real smart soundin' (like Edith). I been tryin' to copy Edith but I get my words mixed up.

I didn't expect to see so many women at the meeting. I figured it would be just the four of us with Dr. Morgan but there was four younger-lookin' women, too. Dr. Morgan welcomed us and said we was to use only first names. We went around the circle and introduced ourselves. Then we said a prayer together. It's called the Serenity Prayer and we read it from a card.

"Yesterday," said Dr. Morgan, "We were discussing self-esteem. What are some ways we can nurture our self-esteem, and why is it important to our recovery?"

One of the younger women—a purty black woman dressed real stylish—spoke up. I think her name was Tressa. "If we don't value ourselves and take care of ourselves in relationships, we can't expect other people to treat us with respect."

"Exactly," Dr. Morgan said. "What are some ways we can take care of ourselves with other people?"

"By setting boundaries?" another woman asked. I don't remember her name.

"That's right. Can you give me an example?" asked the doctor.

"Like if you're on a date and the guy tries to get hands-y and you're not ready," Tressa said.

"Or if your husband wants to have sex and you don't," added another.

"Okay, let's go with that. How would you take care of yourself in that situation?"

"Tell him to stop," suggested Ruth.

"Oh, sure," interjected Julia, "and get your clock rung!"

"Did that happen to you, Julia?" asked Dr. Morgan.

"Too many times to count," she said, her voice dripping with disgust.

"Why did it happen more than once? Why would you go back to a man who hit you and forced you to have sex?"

"I figured I could make him love me and then it wouldn't feel forced. Besides, my father hit my mom all the time. I guess it seemed natural. Once he even forced her to have sex right in front of us kids." Julia looked like she was gonna throw up and I was startin' to feel nauseated, too.

"Here's what you need to understand about an abusive man. While the actual abuse may not be his intention, his objective is to control you, and he thinks he is entitled to it. There are early warning signs but women ignore them because often the relationship starts as idyllic. After a period of grooming the abuse starts in subtle ways. Later, because the woman has been humiliated so often, she thinks no one else could love her."

"Brad was very charming at first," said Julia. "I told everyone what a wonderful man he was. I felt so proud of him. Then, when the subtle behaviors started, I figured I must have done something wrong. I started blaming myself for his put-downs and constant criticism. I was too embarrassed to tell anyone. After we got married the hitting started. I couldn't believe my wonderful husband—whom I adored—would ever lay a hand on me. Even more confusing was the fact that he apologized every time. He even cried and promised it would never happen again. That was four years ago."

"What finally convinced you to leave, Julia?" asked Samantha.

"Brad had gone to bed early with a headache, and I was watching this piece on *Nightline* or *Sixty Minutes*—I forget which one. It sounded like the story of my life. I was shocked to learn that Battered Woman Syndrome was a real condition. I thought I was the only woman whose loving husband flew into a rage at least once a day and beat the crap out of her. For all those years, I was convinced it was my fault whenever he lost control. That very night I started making a plan to leave, and here I am."

"That took tremendous courage, Julia." Dr. Morgan said. "You should be very proud of yourself." Everyone applauded. "Can someone share a situation different from Julia's, yet that still exemplifies abuse?"

"My husband, George, never hit me," said Samantha. "I guess that's why it took me so long to recognize his behavior as abuse."

"How did it manifest, Samantha?" asked Dr. Morgan.

"It started with teasing and mild insults. He would say things like, 'If you were smart you would know that.' His favorite line was, 'I love my cute, dumb blonde.' In social settings, he would introduce me as his 'dumb blonde arm-candy' and give me a big, conspicuous hug. After the first few times this happened I told him it made me feel uncomfortable. He called me a drama queen and insisted I was being overly sensitive. Then he quickly acted like everything was back to normal. 'You know I love you,' he'd say and we'd have make-up sex. It was so confusing."

"Do you see how George was maintaining control over you?" asked Dr. Morgan.

"I do... now."

"Stella, would you like to share anything with the group?" Dr. Morgan asked.

"No, Ma'am," I said, staring at the floor. Oh! I had plenty to say! I wanted to spill my guts about Hank but first I needed to feel safe. I needed to know for sure these women wouldn't judge me or shame me for stayin' with him. No. I weren't ready to share my terrible secrets... not yet.

"Anyone else?" She waited a minute or so before wrappin' up the session. "Okay, then let's recap. What are some of the initial signs of abuse that are easy to miss?"

"Insults, put-downs," somebody said.

"Yes."

"Excuses for their violent outbursts," someone else added.

"Like what?" Dr. Morgan asked.

"Like 'I have a temper. I can't help it'."

"Yes. What else?"

"'If you would only'—fill in the blank—'then I wouldn't get so mad. It's your fault I lose my temper.'"

"Right. Who else has heard that one?" Several hands shot up.

"How about, 'My father beat me or my mother criticized me, so I can't stop myself'?" Tressa asked.

"Yes. Notice how the responsibility always shifts away from the abuser to someone else," explained the doctor.

"'It'll never happen again. I promise,'" Samantha added with a cynical tone. I had to admit I hadn't ever heard that one from Hank. After he started hittin' me he never once apologized. I guess he always thought he had the right.

"Good. Thank you, ladies, for sharing. I'll see you all tomorrow evening." Then she asked me to stay behind. I was sure she was gonna scold me for not speakin' up but she just said—in a real kind voice, "Stella, we need to set up your individual sessions. Could we meet during the day or do you need an evening time?"

"I work till four, and then I'm on dinner duty," I answered.

"How about Saturday mornings for a start? Would ten o'clock work?"

"Yes, Ma'am. Ten is fine," I agreed.

"Okay, we'll have our first session next Saturday at ten a.m."

Jodie

A nice lady, Edith, came to see me and brought me some pretty uh, night-gowns from Stella, and a real doll—not a chicken-bone doll. She brought me my bear that Mama gave me a long time ago. I thought Hank threw it away. I'm so happy to have my bear again. I ain't ever gonna let go of it.

The other ladies—nurses, they're called, just like on General Hospital—well, they been helping me walk. My legs ain't strong. It hurts to walk but they'll get better. The nurses said so. I gotta keep working them to make them stronger.

I like this hospital. The bed is soft and has a warm blanket. There's a television box up on the wall and I can almost see the picture. Nurse Rebecca says my eyes'll get better. They ain't used to the light yet.

I want Stella to come. Edith said she will but she hasn't yet. I hope Hank doesn't come. I don't ever want him to come. Hank hurts me and he hurts Stella. I don't ever wanna go back to that room. Sometimes I dream about it—being chained to the bed and Hank hitting me and being cold at night and hungry, too. In the dream, I scream and scream. Whenever I scream for real the nurses come and help me get calm. They talk real quiet and rub my back. I wish I can stay here for always but I want Stella to come. I hug my bear and my Amy-Doll and try to dream about Stella and Mama.

Mike

The next Saturday evening I picked up Edith at seven. Although we were both casually dressed this time she looked just as gorgeous as she had on our first date. I love it when she wears her hair down around her shoulders like that.

We had decided to get a pizza and then go bowling. I was hoping she would ask me up to her apartment when I took her home but I certainly wasn't about to make the first move. Edith—being such a principled woman—might have a strong opinion about sex outside of marriage. Of course, the way she attacked me in her office last week leads me to believe she wants it as much as I do. A healthy man needs only the hint of an invitation to move the sex-train forward and that performance was more than a hint, in my book. But I surely don't want to jeopardize a future with Edith by insulting her sensibilities. I know I love her and want to marry her. We get along great and always enjoy each other's company. Yeah, I know. It's only our second date but we've known each other for years. We've been friends for a long time, and I think I've always loved her.

Over pizza we talked about the kid. Edith had been to visit Jodie in the hospital. I could tell she cared about the girl. She even picked up a load of gifts for her—clothes and toys and stuff. She said Jodie was walking a little and that she even said a couple of words. She's far from a normal, healthy child. That's for sure. The poor kid even has rickets. I thought rickets disappeared with the horse and buggy. She'll have to be treated for psychological trauma as well as physical injuries and malnutrition but—from what the nurse told Edith—she'll recover, eventually, with the proper treatment.

Talking about Jodie led us to a conversation about kids, in general, and with some hesitation I asked Edith if she wanted to try for another baby one day. She said she had always wanted a family but she was afraid to risk losing another baby. She didn't seem to mind talking about it so I delved a little deeper. "What did your doctor say about the chances of having another miscarriage?"

"She said there was no explanation as to why some babies abort spontaneously, and there was no reason I couldn't have another baby." That's what I had hoped to hear. I definitely want children, and now I'm sure I want Edith to be their mother. At that moment, I realized I was ready to pop the question—but not in a pizza parlor and not until I had the chance to prepare

Edith. I decided I would plan a romantic date for the following weekend. It would give me time to shop for a ring. I could buy it on credit and pay off the balance when I got my promotion. Now, how will I determine her ring size? What if I choose something she hates? Maybe we should pick it out together. What if she says, "No"? Oh, man! Here I go again with my insecurities. I guess I'll figure it out as I go. In the meantime, I need to study hard for that exam.

Anyway, we had lots of laughs at the bowling alley. I threw plenty of gutter balls and Edith threw mostly strikes. She had failed to inform me, in advance, that she used to play on a team and her typical score is two hundred. She trounced me solidly but we had such a great time together, talking and laughing, I didn't care a whit about losing. It didn't hurt that she was wearing those tight jeans either. I could've sat there all night watching her throw strikes.

When we pulled up to Edith's apartment building around eleven, I started to get nervous. We sat in the car for a while and kissed—a lot. I was careful to keep my hands in the safe zones. It took every ounce of restraint on my part. I was determined to give Edith complete control over our physical relationship. I wanted her to trust that my love for her was genuine and not based on lust alone. Finally, Edith called a halt to the necking.

"I had a wonderful time tonight, Mike," she said. "I really like being with you."

"But?" I asked.

"But nothing. I had a wonderful time and I like being with you."

"Oh, good. It seemed like there was going to be a 'but.' I had a wonderful time, too. How about a picnic tomorrow afternoon? It's supposed to be a beautiful day, temperatures in the seventies and sunny all day."

"That sounds great," she agreed. "I want to visit Jodie after church, and I promised Stella I'd stop by the shelter, too. Could we make it a supper picnic?"

"Sure."

"The café closes early on Sundays, so I won't have to rush back for the dinner shift. Shall I have Louie make us some of his fabulous roast beef sandwiches with horseradish and potato salad?"

"Perfect! I'll bring a bottle of wine and stop by that new cupcake place for dessert. What's your favorite flavor?" I asked.

"Well, I never met a cupcake I didn't like, so surprise me, okay?"

"Okay. Dill pickle it is."

"Ha, ha! Very funny," she laughed.

"What time should I pick you up, and where shall we go?"

"How about that beautiful spot down by the lake—you know next to the gazebo? I can call or text you when I get back from seeing Stella."

"Sounds good. I'll see you tomorrow." I reached over and kissed her again—this time very gently—touching only her face. Saying good-bye is getting harder every time. I don't want to spend another minute apart from this woman.

Chapter 16

Edith

I have fallen hard for Sergeant Mike Travers. We had the best time last night. I'm not some star-struck teenager. I'm old enough and experienced enough to recognize the genuine article. I don't know what took me so long to trust my instincts about Mike. Maybe I thought a man who would fall for Libby Marshall's wiles wasn't all that bright... or stable. Now I realize he's just a good guy who got taken advantage of by a two-timing floozy. He deserves so much better. I intend to shower him with love that he can trust.

My original plan for Sunday was to visit Jodie after church and then go to the shelter. I was anxious to report Jodie's progress to Stella. As I left the service, I turned on my cell phone ringer and discovered a shocking message from Mike. Stella had been arrested. I couldn't believe it. She was finally getting her life on track and now this. As soon as I reached my car, I called Mike.

"What happened, Mike?" I asked without preamble.

"It was the social worker, that Ms. Cartwright. She reported Jodie's condition to CPS and they swore out a warrant for Stella's arrest."

"That nurse promised me she'd tell me when the social worker was coming."

"I was the only cop who knew Stella's whereabouts, and I was forced to divulge it. I feel terrible but I had no choice."

"That poor woman. She can't catch a break. Is she there at the station?"

"Yes, for now anyway."

"What's the charge?"

"Child neglect and abuse."

"Oh, Mike! She loves Jodie. She was under the control of that monster, Hank."

"You might know that, but the law sees it differently."

"I'll be right over." With a mixture of emotions churning my stomach into knots, I called the café and then headed to the station. I didn't know if I'd be allowed to see Stella but I knew she needed a friend. Convinced it would take a miracle to help her out of this latest predicament, I prayed the whole way there. She needed God's strength more than ever. A top-notch attorney couldn't hurt, either.

I pulled into the parking lot beside the precinct and rushed to the front of the building. I had never set foot in the police station before. I had no idea what to expect or where to find Mike but I needn't have worried. He was waiting for me just inside the door. I wanted to fall into his comforting embrace and feel his strong arms engulfing me, but I restrained my urge so I wouldn't embarrass him in front of his colleagues. He gave me a quick peck on the cheek and ushered me to a nearby sitting area. I noticed he was out of uniform and remembered it was Sunday, his day off.

"Tell me what happened," I urged as we sat on the edge of a not-so-comfortable sofa across from the drink machine.

"According to Captain Howard, the call came in yesterday afternoon. The social worker—that Ms. Cartwright—went to see Jodie again yesterday and determined the child had been severely neglected and abused for an extended period. I guess she spent the afternoon accumulating information about the case which, of course, led her to Hank and Stella. She got a warrant and the cops on duty picked up Stella at the shelter this morning."

"But, Mike, Stella tried to protect Jodie. It was Hank who..."

"Yes, you and I know... well, we're convinced that Stella wasn't the one who abused Jodie but what proof is there, really? It's just her word against his, and she certainly didn't report him."

"Do you mean Stella could actually be convicted of child abuse? She was being abused, too," I said.

"At the very least, she could be charged as an accessory."

"This is terrible. She was just starting a new life—just getting a chance to... May I see her?"

"I think so. Let me check with the captain." As Mike stood and disappeared through a door labeled "No Admittance," I tried to hold back the tears that were blurring my vision. I knew I had to be strong for Stella—to convince her of my confidence that everything would work out. Somehow, I would find the money to pay her bail. After all she had been through, I couldn't let her spend more than one night in a jail cell.

When Mike returned, he was accompanied by a uniformed officer who motioned me through the door toward the rear of the station. "You have ten minutes with the prisoner," she said. She was dangling a set of keys which she used to open a heavy metal door. Behind the door was a dark corridor flanked on each side by two cells. I guessed that one side was for female prisoners and the other was for males. The first two cells were dark and empty. In the last compartment to the left she sat on the edge of a simple cot holding her head in her hands. Not once did she look up or even acknowledge our presence. Her body language betrayed her utter despair. The cell—furnished with only a bed and a toilet—looked bleak. A barred window at the back threw a sliver of sunlight across the tiny space. The pillow-less bed was covered with an ugly army-green blanket. *This dismal chamber is a far cry from her lovely room at the shelter*, I thought.

As the officer opened the heavy, barred door, I took a deep breath and bit my lip, determined to hold my tears at bay. The door clanked shut behind me, leaving Mike on the other side. "I'll be back in a few minutes," he said. It took only three steps for me to reach the cot where I sat gingerly beside the despondent woman. Placing my hand gently on her back, I remained silent. After a minute or so she reached her arms around my neck and sobbed into my shoulder.

"Oh, Edith," she said. "What am I gonna do?"

"Don't worry, Stella," I assured her. "I'm going to get you out of here just as soon as I can."

"Just when things was startin' to get better."

"I know, but you mustn't give up. We'll find you the best lawyer in the county and we'll prove your innocence."

"What if I never get to see Jodie again and what about Amy? How am I gonna get her outta prison now that I'm behind bars?"

"We'll figure it out, Stella," I said, as I pushed her away gently and took her hands in mine. "You're not alone anymore. You have me and you have Mike. We'll work this out together, and one day soon you and your daughter and granddaughter will be reunited. You'll see." I didn't believe what I was saying any more than she did but I couldn't let her give up hope. There had to be a way to make sure justice was served, and I intended to find it.

Mike

I felt like a heel. Turning in Stella was one of the hardest things I've had to do in my whole career as a cop. I'm just glad the captain didn't send me to pick her up. When Ted brought her in I made myself scarce because I couldn't face the poor woman. At least Edith doesn't blame me. She knows I had no choice.

Edith and I kept our picnic date, but it wasn't exactly the romantic tryst I had hoped it would be. All we talked about was Stella's situation and how we could help. That's okay though. We'll have the rest of our lives together for romance.

We agreed that, for now, we needed to focus our time and energy on getting Stella out of jail and back to work. Edith offered to dip into her savings account to post bail, and I agreed to contact the lawyer who works with a lot of women at the shelter. Her name is Dolly-something and she has an excellent track record. Fredrickson. That's it. Dolly Fredrickson. She has led some domestic abuse training sessions for attorneys and judges throughout the state. I suppose with a name like Dolly you'd have to be top-notch in your field to be taken seriously. I promised Edith I'd get in touch with Ms. Fredrickson first thing Monday morning. When I described Stella's situation Ms. Fredrickson seemed very interested. She didn't promise anything but I got the impression she might take the case pro bono.

Stella's bail hearing was set for ten a.m. Tuesday, which meant another night in jail for her. Edith was determined to attend the hearing. I feared that without legal representation the judge might not release her. I needed to get Ms. Frederickson on the case pronto. She showed up at the station promptly at nine Tuesday morning. After holding a preliminary interview with Stella, she accompanied her to the courthouse. Edith and I were there, too. In my opinion, Dolly's reputation was well-earned. Not more than twenty minutes after our arrival, the judge released Stella into Edith's custody and the two of them were on their way to the café.

Edith and I agreed my next stop would be the Agape Shelter. My job was to make sure Stella still had a place to live until she could get set up on her own. She could always go back to that dump she shared with Hank but it wasn't fit to inhabit. Besides, what if Hank happened to get released on bail or something? He'd kill her for sure.

I wasn't certain the captain would let me off work for the whole morning, but he did. He mentioned that—since Hank's arrest—he had been studying Amy Leonard's case. As a result, he finally agreed it was time to launch a new investigation. He assigned Ted to the case and said I could work with him. I was over-the-moon and couldn't wait to tell Edith about this new development. As soon as I reached my cruiser, I called her cell phone to share the news.

"Mike, that's wonderful," she exclaimed. "Now you won't have to sneak around to gather evidence. Did Ted find anything suspicious in the court transcripts?"

"We can't access the transcripts."

"Why not?"

"It would cost a fortune. Even lawyers have to order them from a private company and the cost is prohibitive."

"So, what's the next step, then?"

"Evidently, Captain Howard has taken a second look at the initial investigation. We're supposed to meet tomorrow morning to plan a strategy. I'm on my way to the shelter to talk to Wendy," I added. "I'll see you later."

"Okay, Mike. Thanks. I can't wait to share your news with Stella."

Stella

I can't get over how good Edith is to me. Just when I think I'm gonna have to stay in that jail for a long time, she comes up with two thousand dollars to bail me out. Someday—if I don't end up in prison—I'm gonna pay her back for all her kindness. That lawyer, Ms. Fredrickson, seems real nice, too, and smart. She acted like she believed everything I told her. She said she couldn't make no promises but she's gonna work real hard to prove I didn't hurt Jodie.

Edith said she'd take me to see Jodie in the hospital after the lunch shift was over. She told me Jodie remembered her bear, even remembered it come from Amy. She said, "Mama" when Edith give it to her. I think Jodie can talk more than she lets on. She's just afraid because of Hank's threats. I can't wait to see her and hug her. Edith says she's doin' real good and gettin' stronger. She's even walkin' some. Maybe she can go to school next fall, and maybe I can take her to see Amy in the prison after a spell. I don't want Amy to see her like she is now, not till she's strong and healthy.

I shoulda reported Hank a long time ago. I didn't know what he was doin' to me was a crime. I just thought them drugs was makin' him mean. I thought if I kept him happy, he wouldn't beat me or Jodie. Listenin' to Dr. Morgan and them other women made me realize I have just as many rights as Hank and maybe I didn't deserve to get beat or hollered at. Lots of times he made me have sex when I didn't want to just like them other women was talkin' about. I thought because we was married I had to do it. I knowed he hated me because of Henry dyin'. The sex surely felt like hate, not love. I couldn't figure how he could make love with someone he hated. Now I know it was another way of controlling me. I can't believe how long I lived like that. But I couldn't run away and leave Jodie there with Hank. Why didn't I call the police? I just don't know. I guess I was scared of losin' Jodie and I weren't—wasn't—thinkin' straight.

I hope Wendy lets me go back to the shelter because I sure don't want to go back to that awful house with all them bad memories. I like them other women at the shelter and I like that Dr. Morgan. I was startin' to feel safe there. At least I can work at the café while I'm waitin' for my trial. I can keep savin' money for a place where Jodie and me can live till Amy gets outta prison. What I can't understand is how come Amy and me has to pay for Hank doin' drugs and Hank beatin' us. It don't make sense.

Chapter 17

Edith

I drove Stella to the café so we could help with the lunch shift and take care of some bills that were nearly overdue. Then we went to the hospital. I still had the toys for Jodie in the back seat of my car. I suggested Stella give them to her and show her how to play with them. I made her promise she would say the gifts were from her.

"Edith, why are you so good to me and Jodie?" she asked.

"Why not?" I answered. "That's what friends do for each other. They help each other."

"But I can't do nothin'—I mean, anything—in return," she said.

"I don't expect anything in return. Someday I might need help and it'll be your turn to be there for me. That's how friendship works."

"I guess I ain't never—haven't never—had a real friend before."

"Haven't ever," I corrected before I realized what I had done. "Oh, sorry. I didn't mean to criticize your speech."

"It's okay. I want to talk better and it helps when you tell me," she said. I breathed a sigh of relief that I hadn't offended her.

"So, I haven't ever," she repeated slowly, "had a real friend. Is that right?"

"Good," I said. "You can also say, I have never."

"Ain't—isn't—that what I said in the first place?" she asked.

"Not quite. You see, haven't is a negative and never is a negative. You don't use two negatives in a row."

"I'll never get used to all them—those—rules but I'll keep tryin'. I almost graduated high school but in the mountains of Tennessee everybody talked the way I do. I know it don't— it doesn't—sound smart and I want Amy to be proud of her mama. She's been gettin' her college education inside the prison. She's startin' to sound real smart. Maybe I can do that, too."

"You're not going to prison, Stella, not if Mike and I have anything to say about it."

"I sure do appreciate what you're doin' for me, and Sergeant Travers, too, but it looks like I'm gonna have to serve some time. I need to be thinkin' straight about it, and I need to make sure Jodie has somebody to take care of her while I'm gone."

"Anyway," I said, anxious to distract her from the subject of imprisonment, "the reason you've never had a real friend has nothing to do with who you are. It's because Hank wouldn't allow it. I'm surprised he even let you work."

"I reckon he knew he wouldn't be able to buy his dope if I didn't work. Leastwise, without my paychecks, we would've been livin' on the street."

We pulled into the hospital parking lot and walked to the entrance. I carried the bag of toys and slowed my usual pace so Stella could keep up with me. We rode the elevator to Jodie's floor and headed for her room. "Hold it," someone called from the nurses' station. It wasn't Rebecca and it wasn't the other nurse whom I had met Saturday. She rushed around the counter to stop us.

"What's the problem?" I asked. "We're here to see Jodie Leonard."

"Are you her grandmother?" she asked me. "I'm not, but she is," I said, motioning to Stella. *If I look old enough to be Jodie's grandmother, it's time for a facelift*, I thought.

"She can't go in," the imposing nurse declared.

"What do you mean she can't go in?" I asked, incredulously. "She wants to see her granddaughter."

"I've been instructed to not let Stella Leonard in to see Jodie."

"Why?" Stella asked. "Why can't I see her? Who says I can't see my Jodie?" She was beginning to raise her voice and push the nurse—who was now blocking the door to Jodie's room—out of the way.

"Hold on, Stella," I said trying to calm her. "There must be some mistake." Then addressing the nurse, I asked, "On whose authority?"

"The child's social worker, Ms. Cartwright. She said to call the police if Stella Leonard showed up here and tried to see the child."

"You've got to be kidding! This is Jodie's grandmother. She has a right to see her granddaughter." Now all three of us were shouting and Stella was trying to move the nurse out of the doorway.

"Jodie! My Jodie!" she cried, managing to push the door open enough that we could see Jodie holding out her arms, reaching for Stella.

"Stella!" she called from her bed, as she reached her tiny arms over the railing toward her grandmother. We were making a huge scene which drew the attention of numerous hospital personnel and visitors.

"Call security," the nurse shouted.

"No, wait," I shouted in return, trying to be heard above the din we had created. I pulled Stella away from the door and tried to calm her. "Okay, okay," I said to the nurse, "There's no need to call the authorities. Let's all just calm down. I need the number for Ms. Cartwright."

In the background, I could hear Jodie crying and calling for Stella. Another nurse entered the room to attend to her. My heart ached for the child and for her grandmother, but I knew we wouldn't get anywhere with force. It would only make matters worse. Stella sank to the floor weeping. Amid the turmoil her cane had been knocked out of her hand. I retrieved it and helped her to her feet. Then I led her to a nearby chair in the lobby. "Stay here," I said. "I'll sort this out and come back for you."

"She needs me. Jodie needs me." Stella sobbed.

"I know, I know, but she'll just get more upset if she sees you like this. Try to be calm. I'll be right back."

Now the nurse returned to her station, but was watching me carefully. As I headed in that direction she bristled. I took a couple of deep breaths and tried to smile. "Listen, Nurse... uh, Reynolds," I said, as I eyed her name tag. "I don't want to cause any trouble. I know you're just doing your job."

"That's right," she said, relaxing a bit. "I have my orders."

"I understand. Could you please just give me Ms. Cartwright's phone number?"

"I suppose that would be okay," she answered. She turned to the computer screen, hit a few keys on the keyboard, and wrote something on a piece of paper. When she handed it to me she said, "Now, you need to remove Mrs. Leonard from this floor or I'll have to call security to escort her."

"Thank you," I said, accepting the note with what I hoped was a submissive-looking countenance. "We're leaving now." I helped a reluctant Stella to the elevator, explaining that we'd stand a better chance of seeing Jodie later if we cooperated now. When we reached the lobby, I suggested we cross the street and find a bench in the park-like area across from the hospital entrance. I promised Stella I'd call Ms. Cartwright and straighten out the mix-up but first I needed to talk to Mike.

"Edith," he explained, "Stella is a suspected child abuser. Of course, Jodie's social worker is going to prevent her from seeing the child."

"But, Mike, you should have heard Jodie crying for Stella. It's as plain as the nose on my face that Jodie needs her and isn't afraid of her. If Stella had been abusing the girl wouldn't she be afraid of her?"

"You know the truth," Mike continued, "but Ms. Cartwright doesn't. She has to do her job—which is to protect Jodie."

"This is a nightmare. I feel like every turn we take is a dead end. Where do we go from here? Do you think I should call Ms. Cartwright?"

"Honestly, no. I think you should let Dolly handle it. She has agreed to take Stella's case and it's up to her to arrange supervised visits with Jodie." As upset and impatient as I was feeling, I trusted Mike's counsel. I dreaded sharing it with Stella, but I trusted it.

"Okay," I agreed, feeling defeated. I had walked away from the bench where I had left Stella examining the bag of toys yet to be delivered. Now I headed back in that direction.

"I do have some good news, though," Mike added before we ended the call.

"I could use some good news and so could Stella."

"I talked to Wendy at the shelter and she assured me Stella's space is secure."

"Well, praise the Lord for that," I exclaimed. Just as I suspected, Mike's advice didn't set well with Stella, but I finally got her to agree it wouldn't help her case if she bucked the system. Reluctantly, we walked to the parking lot.

"I'll drive you to the shelter," I said, sliding into the driver's seat. I've been cleared to go there without an escort."

"I can take the bus. There's a stop right over yonder."

"It's on my way, Stella, and besides, you were released into my custody. But, first we're going to take a little detour for some retail therapy."

"Retail therapy? What's that?" she asked.

"You'll see." I'm quite sure I was smiling as we headed to the mall.

Stella

If Edith hadn't been with me at the hospital, I probably would've decked that nurse to get to Jodie. She was cryin' and I was cryin' and we made a whole big commotion. Edith got me calmed down, though, and we walked outside. While she talked to Sergeant Travers on her cell phone I sat on a bench under a tree. A breeze was blowin' and I could smell honeysuckle in the air. It reminded me of my childhood when Mama and me used to sit on the back porch shuckin' peas. I was holdin' that Target bag and lookin' at the toys Edith bought for Jodie. I wondered if I'd ever be able to give them to her. She ain't—hasn't—had a toy to play with since she was three years old. Edith said she liked her Teddy bear and remembered it was from her mama. Would we ever be together again, the three of us? I felt like givin' up but Edith wouldn't let me. She kept sayin', "Trust God and trust the system. You have a lawyer now and Mike says she's a good one. Let's give her a chance to prove just how good she is."

Edith is helpin' me with my talkin' too. I want to sound smart and make Amy proud of me. I want to get educated just like her, and I want Jodie to go to school.

After we left the hospital Edith drove us to the mall. She said it was time I had some new clothes. I can't remember the last time I shopped for clothes. I ain't never shopped at a mall, that's for sure. I used to buy clothes for Amy and Jodie at the Goodwill. That mall was real purty inside with shiny floors and fancy stores everywhere. Edith took me to the JC Penney store where she said for me to wait in a dressing room. It had a big long mirror in it. I ain't seen myself from top to bottom like that in a long time and I didn't like what I saw. The woman starin' back at me was old, tired, and sad-lookin'. No wonder Amy looked so shocked when she saw me.

I sat on the bench and waited. Finally, Edith come back and she was carrying a load of clothes for me to try on. "I estimated your size," she said, all excited-like, "but if these don't fit I can bring a different size. Here. Try this one first. I think the colors are perfect for your complexion." She handed me a real purty dress in pinks and purples and hung the other clothes on a hook. "I'll wait outside," she said. "Tell me when you have it on."

"No, don't go," I pleaded. "I think I'm gonna need your help. I ain't sure which way this goes."

"Sure. Okay, let's get your blouse off and slip this over your head. The zipper goes in the… Oh my God!" she said when I pulled off my top. I glanced up at the mirror to see her shocked expression. She was staring at my back with eyes as big as saucers.

"Oh, Stella!" She looked like she seen a ghost. As she turned me around to face her, I could see her eyes starting to tear up. Now I was feelin' embarrassed because Edith was slowly lookin' me up one side and down the other. She slumped down on the bench like her legs wouldn't hold her. When I realized she done seen my bruises and scars—I guess I was so used to them I forgot about how awful they must look—I tried to cover my nearly-naked body with my hands. "How have you survived it?" she asked weakly—like she had the breath knocked outta her.

"I had to for Jodie," I answered.

"Never again, Stella. Hank will never again lay a hand on you or Jodie. I'll make sure of that." She stood and hugged me easy—like I would break—and wiped her tears. "Come on, let's see how this looks on you. No. Wait. I have an idea." She started fishin' around frantically in her purse and pulled out her cell phone. "What we have here is evidence. Cold, hard evidence. Would you mind if I took some pictures?"

"Pictures? Pictures of my naked body?" I said, as I covered my breasts.

"Pictures of your bruises."

"One of them workers at the shelter already done that, as soon as I checked in," I said. "I felt ashamed for her to see me like that, but she was real kind and didn't act shocked at all."

"Oh, of course they would take photos for evidence. That's good. I wish I had a picture of your black eyes and fat lip when Hank broke your nose," Edith said.

"I ain't lettin' him do it again just so you can take a picture." We both laughed at that and went back to our task of gettin' me some new clothes. When we left the JC Penney, Edith had used her credit card to buy me a purty dress, a pair of jeans, two tops, and some slacks. She also made me get some bras and panties. I ain't owned a bra since I was in my twenties.

I can't believe how good Edith is to me. I feel like a movie star or somethin' the way she spends money on me and Jodie. I'll pay her back someday. You can just bet on that. 'Course, I won't be wearin' none of these here purty clothes if I go to prison.

After we finished shoppin', Edith drove me to Agape House and said she'd pick me up for work in the mornin' if I was ready to start back at the café. She said there weren't—wasn't—no—any—point in me ridin' the bus since it was on her way. That'll save me some more money that I can put away for a new place to live. I still wanted to see Jodie somethin' awful but, leastwise, I had a place to live for now. All them women welcomed me back like I was the prodigal daughter. Maybe they didn't know I got arrested. I wore my new slacks and one of my new tops to dinner. I wore that bra too. Ruth and Samantha said I looked real nice.

After I finished vacuuming, I joined the group session. They had got started but they stopped to say, "Hi, Stella." I already felt at home here because everybody was so friendly and nice.

"Sorry I'm late," I said, taking a seat in the circle. "I had to finish my chores."

"It's okay, Stella," said Dr. Morgan. "We're just getting started. Tonight, our subject is legal resources for battered women. I have some handouts that many of you will find helpful. Please pass them around the circle. Now, let's talk about restraining orders. Has anyone here been successful in obtaining a restraining order against your abuser?"

"I have a restraining order against my husband, but it hasn't stopped him," Samantha said. "That's why I had to come here."

"Tell us about that, Samantha."

"My lawyer managed to get him out of the house, but he kept returning. The first time I stupidly took him back. He begged and begged and swore he loved me. He promised he'd never lay a hand on me again. He said he knew he had a problem with anger and promised he'd get counseling."

"How did that go?" asked Dr. Morgan.

"Everything was great for about two weeks, I guess. He was extra attentive and sweet, like the man I thought I married."

"And then?"

"One night I was about thirty minutes late coming home from work. I had called him from the car to let him know I hit some traffic. There was no answer so I left a message. I guess he never got it. The second I stepped into the house from the garage, he grabbed me and threw me to the floor. He was in a rage—accusing me of having an affair and calling me a 'wicked whore'. He started kicking me and insisting I name my 'many sexual partners'. Every time I tried to stand up he slapped my face and knocked me down again. I was scooting backwards into the kitchen like a trapped animal. I was trying to cover my face with one arm and find some kind of weapon with the other. Without realizing what I was doing, I was heading toward the knife drawer. I had never fought back before, but this time I was livid. How dare he woo me back with his fake declarations of love and false promises of getting therapy! Never again would I trust him. Suddenly the adrenaline coursing through my body gave me the strength to lean back and kick him in the knee, knocking him off balance. As he grabbed his injured knee and hopped on the other leg, he fell backward. That's when I jumped up—feeling absolutely no pain—and reached into the drawer for the biggest knife I could find. He was stunned momentarily both by my unprecedented behavior and from hitting his head on the metal trash can. I grasped the opportunity to fling knives at him with my left hand, one-after-the-other, while I maintained a tight hold on the butcher knife in my right hand. Most of the blades missed him but one steak knife gashed his arm as he tried to deflect it. Lunging at him with the butcher knife, I was screaming for him to get out and never come back. He must have believed I meant business because he turned, ran out of the kitchen, and stumbled toward the front door with me and that butcher knife right behind him. As he tried to open the door I landed a solid kick to his behind sending him head-first into the door jamb. I must say, it felt good to be the aggressor for a change. As charged up as I was with both anger and betrayal, I probably could have wrestled a steer to the ground."

Like the rest of us, Ruth was perched on the edge of her chair, listening intently. "What happened next?" she asked.

"Lickety-split I locked that door, ran upstairs, locked myself in the bedroom, and called the cops. I didn't know if he had his keys with him or not. I was shaking so hard I could barely manage to dial 911. When I heard his car pull away, I crumbled on the bed like a dish rag. It was then that I started feeling every slap, punch, and kick he had inflicted. The next morning, I could scarcely move."

"Anyway, when the police came, I gave them my statement and a description of his car. They picked him up at a drug store where he had gone to get some bandages for his arm. They hauled him off to jail but he was out by the next afternoon. While he was behind bars, I called a locksmith to change all the locks on the house, and I contacted a lawyer."

"Did he leave you alone after that?" Tressa asked.

"Oh, no. I even had my land line disconnected. He'd get drunk and hang out on the front porch yelling and crying. I called the police again and again. Twice they arrested him but, both times, he was out by the next day. My lawyer said I should keep filing reports until his multiple violations added up to a felony charge. In the meantime, he started following me and harassing me at work. My lawyer went back to court and filed a 'motion for contempt'."

"Did that help?" asked Dr. Morgan.

"He was charged a fine and jailed for three months. As soon as he got out it started all over again. That's when I came here. Of course, I had to quit my job, a job I loved and needed. I can't sell the house because it's in his name. I can't afford my lawyer anymore. I can't even afford to file for a divorce."

"Unfortunately, ladies, Samantha's story is not unusual," said Dr. Morgan. "But there is help available and that's why we're here. Our priority is to make sure you are safe. After your safety, and the safety of your children, is secure we then move forward with empowering each of you to prepare a strong case with or without an attorney. There are state and national organizations that can be of assistance, too. You'll find many of them listed and described in the pamphlets I distributed earlier. Please take the time to read them and become informed of your legal rights and recourses in this state. Remember this, ladies. Knowledge is power. You can use the legal system to your advantage, but each of you must form a plan of action, according to your individual circumstances."

"Some of you already have peer counselors. If not, let Wendy know you want one assigned to you. A peer counselor can decipher confusing legal terminology, prepare you for court cases, and help you plan your future. If you already have a lawyer, your peer counselor can work with him or her and can even accompany you to court."

"What if your abuser is a high-powered lawyer?" asked Julia.

"Yes, that poses a unique challenge," Dr. Morgan said. "Let's talk about it in your private session tomorrow, Julia. Our session for this evening has come to an end. I'll see you all tomorrow night."

I was learnin' so much from these group sessions. Until I come—came—to this here shelter I thought I was the only woman whose husband hit her. Now I don't feel so alone no more—anymore. When Samantha was talkin' about her husband, I kept rememberin' all the times Hank called me names and hit me. As I listened, I was gettin' madder and madder. Now I knowed he didn't have any right to do that. I could've called the cops and got him put in jail. All them times the cops come—came—to the door I should've told them about Hank. But he would've hit me worse when he got out. Also, if the cops found Jodie… I don't know. I'm still confused. Maybe when I have my private session with Dr. Morgan she can help me figure it all out. I'm supposed to meet with that Ms. Fredrickson soon, too. At least here at the shelter I know I'm not alone. There's other women who understand what I been goin' through and they don't think I'm trash.

Jodie

Stella came yesterday, but that mean nurse wouldn't let her in my room. I cried and Stella cried but it didn't help. I don't understand. I want Stella to come in this room. I want her to hold me. Ms. Edith was trying to help Stella but the nurse made them go away. One of the nice nurses came and hugged me and helped me stop crying. Then I hugged my bear real tight and went to sleep to keep from feeling sad like I used to feel all the time in the dark room.

I'm getting better, though—not so sick feeling—and I can walk better, too. There's a playroom down the hallway a piece. I walked all the way there one day with my walker. That lady—Ms. Cartwright that talks and talks and asks lots of questions—she took me there. Well, I never saw such a place! It was filled with toys just like on commercials. Other kids were there, too. Some had walkers like me and some sat in chairs with wheels. Mostly I watched because I wasn't sure what to do. One kid was riding a—I ain't sure—some animal—not a real animal. It had wheels. Ms. Cartwright asked me did I want to try but I was scared. "That's okay," she said. "Maybe another day."

She asked me did I want to sit on the floor and build with some blocks. She sat and started piling the blocks up but I was looking at a pretty, pink and purple house in the corner. "Shall we go over there?" she asked me. I nodded my head "yes" and pushed my walker to the house. Ms. Cartwright said it was a castle. I remembered that word from *Daniel Tiger's Neighborhood*, but I didn't know a castle looked like this. Castles are where princesses live.

"Would you like to go inside?" Ms. Cartwright asked. She opened the door but when I looked inside it was little and kinda dark. I didn't want to go in. I made up my mind my room down the hall was a better house for a princess. When I turned to go back to my room I started screaming. I couldn't help it because of a bad man standing there. Every time I see one of those men I think Hank is coming for me and I get real scared. The other kids must've got scared too because they started screaming like me. Ms. Cartwright picked me up and grabbed my walker, too. She carried me away from the bad man. She took me back to my room and helped me get calm. I hugged my bear and breathed real deep like nurse Rebecca taught me. When I stopped shaking, Ms. Cartwright asked me the same questions she's been asking like, "What made you afraid?" I don't like talking about Hank but this time I whispered his name.

"Tell me about Hank," she said.

I shook my head, "no," wishing I hadn't even said his name out loud.

"Did Hank hurt you, Jodie?" she asked.

I was afraid if I talked, Hank would come back and get me. I nodded "yes" and checked the door to see if he was outside.

"Hank is in prison, Jodie. He can't hurt you anymore."

"Stella," I whispered.

"Did Stella hurt you?"

I shook my head "No." "Stella come," I said a little louder and started crying.

"You want Stella to come to the hospital?" she asked. I nodded again. "Are you afraid of Stella?"

I shook my head "No."

"Okay, Jodie. I'll see what I can do." I hugged my bear real tight and went to sleep.

Mike

I couldn't wait to tell Edith what Ted and I had discovered in Amy's folder, but I didn't want to get her hopes up until we checked it out thoroughly. We spent two whole days combing through the files. I was determined to find something that would justify either reopening the case or petitioning for Amy's early parole. I even skipped lunch at the café both days. Edith probably suspected something was up.

What she didn't know was that I had been spending my lunch hours planning our "proposal" date. Now that I felt confident Edith loved me as much as I loved her, I was determined to surprise her. First, I went to Sam's Jewelers and picked out a ring. The clerk said to get one that seemed a little big and it could be sized to fit her. "What if she doesn't like it?" I asked.

"You can return it and let her pick out something she likes," he assured me. "Just be sure to keep the box and all of the paperwork." I had to take out an insurance policy in case anything should happen to it, but I would be able to cancel it if I needed to return the ring. Well that settled it. I decided on what's called a "pear shape" diamond with a silver band. The stone wasn't huge but I thought it was pretty. I hoped Edith would like it. I charged it to my credit card. Maybe I shouldn't have, but I was feeling confident I'd be able to start paying it off as soon as my promotion came through.

Since our first date had been at Bonvivant, I made a reservation there for Saturday night. I requested the same table on the veranda and ordered champagne. If I failed my lieutenant's exam, I'd be "up the creek without a paddle," as the saying goes. I had been studying every chance I got and was feeling reasonably confident.

Now that everything was set for Saturday night, I could concentrate on Amy's case. Ted had done some digging that identified the prosecuting attorney for Amy's trial and he interviewed the guy. It seems there was a witness whose testimony had been deemed inadmissible because he was homeless at the time and had a history of mental illness. The prosecutor admitted his strategy had been to prove the witness incompetent to testify. If the public defender, Ms. Thomason, had objected, however, the judge would have been obligated to conduct a competency hearing. According to the prosecutor, Ms. Thomason said nothing.

Ted and I hoped that if we could locate this witness and request a competency hearing his testimony might be admissible, after all. Of course, we had to find him first. Then we had to get Ms. Fredrickson to convince a judge to order a competency hearing. It was a long shot but the right attorney could argue that Gloria Thomason screwed up Amy's defense and declare a mistrial.

Unfortunately, we had only a name, Robert Grogan, to get us started. The prosecutor said Grogan claimed to have been sleeping in the doorway of an abandoned building just a few feet from where the deal took place. The arresting cops picked him up after they cuffed Amy and the dealers. Grogan swore he heard everything that went down that time and during previous transactions, as well.

First, Ted and I went to the scene of Amy's arrest, a spot that has always been popular with the indigent population. It's quite secluded because the abandoned building on the property is covered with vines and surrounded by thick underbrush. We talked to a couple of scraggly looking men but neither had ever heard of Robert Grogan. As I looked around, it occurred to me that Amy must have been terrified to be sent to such a creepy area—not just once, but many times. The heavy growth of bushes and weeds could hide any number of potential attackers. A young woman entering this part of town alone could easily have fallen prey to robbery, rape, or abduction.

Next, we hit the shelter on Camden Boulevard, but it was another dead end. The soup kitchen at St. Mary's was our next stop. There, we were told that they don't require people to give their names, nor do they keep any records of who they serve.

Finally, Ted and I decided to split up. He would head to the hospital's mental health ward and then to the county office to comb through six years' worth of death records. I would visit the social services office and the Salvation Army headquarters. If nothing turned up, we would be forced to admit Robert Grogan had somehow managed to leave the area. I sincerely hoped he was still alive.

It felt like Saturday night would never come, so I was glad to be kept somewhat distracted by the investigation. When the evening finally arrived, I was a nervous wreck. I wanted everything to be perfect for my proposal to Edith. After picking up a half-dozen red roses from the flower shop, I showered and shaved. I brushed my teeth (twice) and gargled with mouthwash. Then, I checked and double-checked my tie, rehearsed my speech, and called the restaurant twice (once to verify my reservation and again to make sure the champagne had been put on ice). Finally, I checked my pocket for the ring and retrieved the vase of roses from the refrigerator. Despite all that, I still arrived at Edith's apartment ten minutes early.

Since my limited understanding of women includes the notion that they don't like their dates to arrive early, I walked up and down the hallway outside her door several times before ringing the bell. I had also heard that when you bring a woman flowers, you should include a vase. Well, maybe that only applies to a dinner party where the hostess is too busy with preparations to hunt for a vase. A tutorial on how to keep the vase from tipping over in the car would have been useful. Seeing no other alternative, I propped it between my legs where it tipped anyway, and created a wet spot on my trousers exactly where a man wouldn't welcome a wet spot—another reason to walk the halls before ringing the doorbell.

When Edith opened the door, she took my breath away. She was wearing a deep blue low-cut dress that made her eyes sparkle like the sapphires on her earlobes. "Hi, Mike," she said as I handed her the roses. "You're right on time. Thank you. These are beautiful and you remembered the vase. I'm impressed." When she took the flowers from me and kissed me with those perfectly luscious lips, I got a whiff of her perfume. It was intoxicating.

"You look—and smell—fabulous, Edith." I said.

"Thanks. You said to dress up. Is this okay?"

"More than okay."

"Oh, good. Come in. I just need to get my shoes and bag. Thanks for the roses. They're my favorite."

"So, where are we going?" she called over her shoulder as she headed toward the bedroom.

"It's a surprise," I answered, glancing around at her neat, tastefully furnished apartment. "I like your place."

"Thanks. I've been here about five years." She returned carrying sparkly silver heels and a small matching purse. "It's just right for one person, and all of my neighbors are great."

You won't be living alone for much longer if I my plans work out.

"Is it still warm outside or should I take a wrap?" she asked.

"The less of that dress you cover, the better," I said, eyeing her lasciviously.

"Why, thank you, Sergeant Handsome," she said, caressing my cheek seductively. Since Edith wasn't prone to flirting, I enjoyed it, all the more, when she did.

"All right," she said, as she locked the door behind us. "But you had better be prepared to give up your jacket if I get cold."

"You bet." As we drove to the restaurant, I updated Edith about Amy's case and she told me what happened at the hospital. It seemed like both of us had hit a wall regarding the Leonard women. But I was determined not to let anything compromise my optimistic mood. I was about to ask Edith Bowman to marry me, and I wanted the evening to be as romantic and carefree as possible.

When we came within a couple blocks of Bonvivant, I instructed Edith to close her eyes. "What are you up to, Sergeant?" she asked.

"Nothing sinister, Ms. Bowman. I just want it to be a surprise. No peeking, okay?"

"Okay," she agreed. I drove around the block once and then circled the next block before turning into the restaurant's parking lot.

"We're here, but keep your eyes closed," I instructed, as I shut off the engine.

"Am I going to have to eat dinner with my eyes closed? How do I know you won't slip me some escargot or pigs brains or something?"

"Just humor me a little longer." I helped her out of the car and took her by the elbow. I had made prior arrangements with the maître d' to enter the veranda through the back gate. So, I steadied Edith along a brick walkway behind the restaurant, through the gate, and to "our" table beside which the champagne was chilling. So far, the evening was turning out perfectly. I held Edith's chair for her and helped her sit. Once she was seated I instructed her to open her eyes.

"Mike. You devil. I had no idea where we were. You really surprised me."

"Do you like it?"

"Of course, but it's so expensive. You can't afford…"

"Tonight," I interrupted, "We're not going to think about the cost. I'll be getting a sizable raise soon and I want the evening to be special."

"It's already special because we're together," she said, settling in.

"At our table, I might add."

"It is our table, isn't it? And is that champagne?"

"May I pour a little bubbly for the lovely lady?"

"You may, indeed." Just then, our waiter approached. He uncorked the bottle and filled the glasses for us. The nervously awaited time had come and I felt like my heart was beating out of my chest. Surely the couple at the next table could hear it pounding.

"I'd like to propose a toast," I started, my voice cracking like that of a seventh-grade boy. "But first, I want to say something, okay?"

"Of course, Mike. What is it?"

As we set our glasses on the table, the waiter backed away, and I took Edith's hand in mine. "Edith, I think I knew I loved you the first time we met… and now that I've gotten to know you, I'm sure of it. You're everything a man could want in a woman," I continued recalling my carefully prepared speech. "You're beautiful, intelligent, kind, and… sexy as hell." That last part wasn't in my original speech but it sure was true. "What I'm trying to say is I want us to be together always." At that point, I slid off my chair onto one knee and pulled the ring box from my breast pocket. Everyone seated on the veranda was staring at us but I didn't care. "Edith Bowman," I asked, as I nearly drowned in those deep blue eyes, "Will you be my wife?"

The next few moments were a blur. She must have said "yes" because somehow the ring ended up on her finger and we were kissing amidst enthusiastic applause. It wasn't until we sat again that I could relax a bit.

"Did you just agree to marry me?" I asked.

"I did. Oh, Mike! I couldn't be happier. What a romantic—perfect—proposal. The ring is beautiful and it fits. How did you... how will you pay...?"

"Don't spoil the evening with practicality. Let's just enjoy it, okay?"

"Okay," she acquiesced.

"Now for that toast. To us and our long and happy marriage." I think we both smiled throughout dinner. We finished the bottle of champagne and I called a cab to take us to Edith's apartment. I wasn't sure how I'd get my car in the morning, but neither of us was in any shape to drive.

"Are you sure about this?" I asked once we were inside.

"Mike, we're two mature adults in a committed relationship. We love each other and we're going to be married. I couldn't be more sure." I kissed my fiancée hungrily and carried her to her bedroom.

Chapter 18

Edith

Mike Travers swept me off my feet Saturday night. He planned a perfectly romantic marriage proposal. I must admit I didn't expect it quite this soon but, as I told him, we're both mature adults who have been married before. We know what we want in a spouse and we know we've found it in each other. Why wait?

Sunday mornings I don't have to be at the restaurant until ten o'clock for the eleven o'clock brunch. I usually attend the early church service but I slept right through it. When I awoke at eight-fifteen, I slid out of bed as quietly as possible. I made coffee and took a quick shower. Mike was just stirring when I crawled back under the covers and handed him a mug of the aromatic brew. "Hey, sleepyhead," I said, as I kissed him gently on the forehead. Since I had left the draperies open all night, bright sunlight was streaming through the window. "It looks like a beautiful day out there."

"It looks like a beautiful day in here," he said sleepily, unfastening my robe.

"Not if you spill coffee all over my new comforter, Sergeant. Now sit up and take your medicine."

"Did you agree to marry me last night or did I dream it?" he asked, accepting the hot mug cautiously.

All in one excited breath, I told him how happy I was and how much I appreciated the effort he had put into his proposal and how much I loved my ring and how much I loved him. "I plan to put as much effort into keeping you happy for a lifetime," he said.

"I was sure I could never love again after Charlie," I said, sipping the hot coffee, "but now I know it's possible to find more than one soulmate in a lifetime."

"I have no intention of trying to replace Charlie, and I don't want you ever to feel uncomfortable talking about him in front of me."

"Thank you, Mike. I'm very blessed," I said as I placed our half-empty cups on the night stand.

After a less-urgent rendition of the previous night's activity we spent the next half hour holding each other and planning our future together. We agreed upon an intimate ceremony at my church followed by a small reception at the café. We still needed to set a date and decide where to live but, those decisions would have to wait. Too soon it was time for me to leave for the café. First, I had to drive Mike back to Bonvivant to retrieve his car—which we hoped hadn't been towed.

Stella

I had my first private session with Dr. Morgan Saturday morning. I was real nervous because I don't know her that well and because I feel shy talkin' about personal stuff with strangers. It weren't—wasn't—all that bad though. Dr. Morgan was so nice and she made me feel easy right away. She knew just the right questions to get me talkin' so I ended up tellin' her about Hank and Amy and Jodie, too. She said she's heard about every kind of abusive situation and she made me feel like I ain't—I'm not—crazy or stupid. It's like when I talk to Edith. She makes me feel like I'm worth somethin' and so does Dr. Morgan.

The doctor told me she thought Hank had three problems makin' him act the way he did. First was his upbringin'. She said if a man gets beat by a parent he's likely to grow up the same way, thinkin' it's normal. Hank told me his daddy beat him and beat his mama and brothers, too. I asked Dr. Morgan why it took him more than five years to start hittin' me. She said Henry's death was so traumatic—that means upsettin'—that the grief triggered Hank's control issues. That was his second problem. He didn't know how to express his grief and didn't have anybody showin' him how. So, he got mad and violent to keep from feelin' sad.

"What was his third problem?" I asked her.

"He turned to self-medication with drugs and alcohol," she said. "That path, naturally, led to addiction." It all made so much sense the way the doctor explained it.

"I kept thinkin' it was my fault," I told her. "I thought if I could keep him from gettin' upset, he'd stop hurtin' us."

"How did that work for you?" she asked.

"Not so good."

"Right. You see, Stella," the doctor said, "that's part of the abuser's method to maintain control. If he kept you blaming yourself, you would continue trying to please him and he could justify his behavior."

Then I asked her, "So, should I forgive him because he couldn't help it?"

"That's your choice, Stella. If you're able to forgive him after all the suffering he has caused, you're a very strong and admirable woman. However, forgiving is not the same as forgetting. You must never forget the pain Hank has inflicted upon you and your daughter and granddaughter because it's your responsibility to protect yourself and them from him. If he should be released from prison—even if he comes out drug-free—your lives could be in danger. If he begs you to take him back, if he declares his love and promises he'll never hit you again, you mustn't trust him. The statistics are not in your favor. I've seen it happen again and again. If you ever let yourself trust him again all three of you could end up dead."

I really had to do some thinkin' on that. I knowed—knew—what Hank was capable of doin' and even though, now I understood why he done them things, I had to make sure Amy and Jodie was always safe from him. Once I got Amy outta prison, I'd move us far away from this here town and maybe change our names, too. But I don't want to move away from Edith and my new friends at the shelter. I hope Hank stays in prison for a long, long time.

Edith called me here at the shelter Sunday afternoon. She said she couldn't wait till Monday to tell me her news. She and Sergeant Travers is—are—gettin' married. He gave her a ring and everything. I'm so happy for her. She deserves to be with a good man like Sergeant Travers. I can tell by the way he looks at her, he's crazy in love with her. If every man was like the sergeant there wouldn't be no need for battered women shelters. He's what you call a true gentleman.

I been tryin' to phone Amy at the prison to tell her about her daddy goin' to prison, but she won't talk to me. Her blamin' me for not protecting her and Jodie is another reason for me thinkin' it was my fault. I want to tell her about Sergeant Travers lookin' into her case and how confident I feel that he can get her out of prison.

I'm supposed to meet with that Ms. Fredrickson tomorrow. She's the lawyer for my case. Sergeant Travers said I don't have to pay nothin'. She's doin' it for free. I have a lot of nice people to pay back someday. Anyway, I need to ask her if she can get me in to the hospital to see Jodie and what's gonna happen to Jodie after she gets outta there. I know she needs a good home and someone to take proper care of her, but I miss her somethin' awful. If she goes to a foster home I might never see her again, and what will I tell her mama? How will I explain to Amy why she got took away from me? Edith keeps tellin' me to think positive but sometimes I just don't feel no—any—hope.

Mike

I'm about the happiest, luckiest guy in the whole world. I've been reeling with joy ever since I proposed to Edith Saturday night and she said "yes." I hope she truly likes the ring. She said it was perfect but she might have been trying to spare my feelings. I wish I could afford a bigger stone. I'd buy the Eiffel Tower for Edith if I could. The important thing is she wants to marry me. Edith Bowman wants to spend the rest of her life with me. I'm relieved she agreed to a small wedding. I'd be nervous in front of a whole big crowd. Besides, with both of us being so caught up with Stella and Amy, we're too busy to plan an elaborate affair. Also, my lieutenant's exam is next week. I need that promotion and the salary that comes with it.

When I reported for work Monday morning, Ted was just finishing a call. He said it was about a lead on Robert Grogan. It turns out we were looking in all the wrong places. According to Ted's source at the Social Security Administration, Grogan is no longer homeless and actually has a job at the service station just off Exit 23.

I was about to pour my second cup of coffee when Ted said to keep my jacket on. We were headed out via the interstate to have a chat with Mr. Grogan. When we got there, we found him working under the belly of a Ford Taurus.

"Robert Grogan?" Ted asked.

"Yeah," he said, eyes focused upward on his work. "I'll be done here in about twenty minutes. You'll have to wait your turn."

"Mr. Grogan," Ted continued, showing his badge, "I'm Inspector Ted Forrest and this is Sergeant Mike Travers."

Now Grogan stepped from beneath the vehicle, stood to face us and wiped his greasy hands on a shop rag. "I can assure you that I—" he started to say.

"Mr. Grogan," Ted interrupted. "You're not in any trouble. We're investigating a case from three years ago, and we're hoping you can help us. Is there someplace private we can talk?"

"Let me check with my boss. Maybe he'll let me take my break early. Come on inside." We entered the office portion of the station where Grogan motioned for us to sit. "Help yourselves to the coffee," he said. "I'll be right back."

By the time we had our coffees creamed, sugared, and stirred, he was back. "The boss says we can use his office. So, what's this about?" he asked, as he poured a cup of the stale brew for himself.

Ted asked him if he remembered Amy Leonard's case when he had been called as a witness. "Yeah, of course." he answered. "I felt sorry for the poor kid. I wanted to testify but that shyster prosecutor wouldn't let me. Said I wasn't a fit witness because I was down on my luck."

"Can you tell us what you saw the day Amy was arrested?" I asked.

"That wasn't the first time. She came to that same spot every week, but I didn't know she was a girl until the cops told me. She dressed like a boy and wore a toboggan or a baseball cap to cover her hair. I guess she thought she'd be safer in that part of town if she looked like a boy. I had a good spot in an alcove of that old abandoned building where I slept at night. You see, I was homeless then." Ted and I nodded but didn't say anything.

"Anyway, every Saturday morning Amy would meet these two crack dealers. I always stayed perfectly still and I could hear every word. Amy did an amazing job of acting and sounding like a guy. One time she showed up with the usual wad of money and the punks announced they had raised the price. 'Overhead, you know,' I heard one of them say. Amy got upset and said her father would kill her if she came home without his dope. That's how I knew she was being forced to buy his drugs. That's what I told the cops and that's what I told Amy's lawyer. The creeps told her to come back that night with fifty bucks more. She begged them—asking if she could buy a smaller bag— but they sent her away empty-handed, said they couldn't split a bag."

"Did she return later?" Ted wanted to know.

"Oh, yeah, but she was messed up."

"What do you mean, 'messed up'?" I asked.

"She was limping pretty badly, and I could tell her face was swollen and bruised."

"You could see that much detail from your spot?"

"Yeah. She always carried a small flashlight. It was dark even during the day because of the thick underbrush. When I peeked around the corner the light shone on her face for a couple of seconds. It was just long enough for me to see that somebody had beat her bad. She looked like she had faced off with a prize fighter."

"Why didn't you contact the police then?"

"Hey, man, I was in a bad way at that time, just trying to survive, myself. The cops would have arrested me and sent me to jail or a psych ward for sure. I had already lost everything—my job, my wife, my home. Everything."

"Why was that, Mr. Grogan?"

"It's no secret. I have a mental illness. It's called paranoid schizophrenia. But I didn't know what it was at the time. I just knew I heard voices and was convinced those voices were trying to control my mind. I thought my wife was conspiring with the cops to kill me. I was hiding out in the woods and just trying to survive."

"So, that's why you weren't allowed to testify?"

"Right."

"You seem fine now," I said. "What happened?"

"Getting arrested the morning of the drug bust was what saved me. After spending a couple nights in jail, I was referred to a mental health professional who diagnosed my illness and started me on a comprehensive treatment program. After a couple months in the hospital, I was released to a group home. Finally, about three months ago, I was able to land this job. I'm a college graduate with a degree in engineering."

"How did you make it through college?" I asked.

"That's the strange thing about schizophrenia. Sometimes it doesn't show up until young adulthood. A few times during college I heard voices but I was so focused on my education and my girlfriend I chalked them up to stress and lack of sleep. Listen. I need to get back to work but I know what I saw and heard that morning and all the other mornings. I know I wasn't hallucinating."

"Are you still willing to testify if we can have you approved as a witness?"

"Absolutely. What happened to that kid, anyway?"

"She has spent the last three years in prison," I said.

"Oh, God! That is not right," he declared. "Do you think you can get her released?"

"Maybe, with your help," Ted said. "Would you mind if we talked to your psychiatrist?"

"Not at all," he answered. "His name is Dr. Southern. His practice is on Ridgewood Drive but he also works at the hospital. I'll call him later and tell him to answer any questions you need to ask. He'll assure you that my condition is being well managed."

"Okay, we'll be in touch," said Ted.

"Thank you for your time, Mr. Grogan, and good luck," I added. As we started to shake hands, he pulled his hand away quickly and wiped it on his coveralls.

"Sorry," he said, as he ushered us out. "Sometimes I forget I'm a grease monkey."

On our way back to the station, Ted and I laid out a plan. The first step was to contact Dr. Southern. That was my assignment. Armed with fresh information and a possible witness, Ted would work on acquiring a new attorney for Amy. Hopefully, he or she would be able to set a retrial or at least a successful probationary release for a young woman who shouldn't have spent one day in prison in the first place.

Jodie

That nice doctor-lady came to see me again. She said I was getting strong and healthy. She said I can get out of this hospital soon but I don't want to go. I want to stay here and I want Stella to stay here, too. Ms. Cartwright says Stella can come to see me. That makes me happy. I want Stella to hold me. My bear's soft fur feels good but Stella's skin feels better.

Yesterday, some other lady came to give me some tests. She showed me lots of pictures and told me to point to stuff. It was fun. She said I was smart and she knew I could talk, but she told me I don't have to talk till I'm ready.

Nurse Rebecca—and sometimes Ms. Cartwright—takes me to the playroom every day. First, they make sure there's no mean men in there so I won't scream. I like the bouncy horse best. I bounce and bounce till it feels like I'm flying. My bear likes to bounce on the horse, too. I got mad and cried when a kid was bouncing on my horse. Rebecca said I had to wait my turn. I didn't like to wait but she played a game with me on the table. It was Chutes and Ladders.

One day, I walked five steps with no walker. Then, I fell down. The next day I walked eight steps. Sadie, my physical therapist, says I can run soon but I don't remember how. Amy used to run with me in that backyard with all the trees. I remember it was fun, but my legs don't remember how to run. I want Amy to come to this hospital. Amy is my mama. Stella said Amy is my mama. I want Amy to come and Stella, too.

Chapter 19

Edith

Mike—my fiancé, Mike, that is—came to breakfast yesterday bearing great news. He said he and Ted had found the witness that hadn't been allowed to testify at Amy's trial. Mike said this guy—Grogan—has information to prove Amy was being forced to buy drugs for Hank. Evidently, Grogan has a mental illness that was untreated at the time but now he's on medication and Mike said he seems reliable.

When I told Stella the good news, she wasn't excited in the least. In fact, she acted depressed. "Amy won't take my calls," she said. "I can't tell her good news or bad news, either cause she won't talk to me."

"I think it's time we went back to that prison, Stella," I asserted.

"She won't agree to see me."

"Maybe I should go alone. Do you think she'd talk to me?"

"I don't know. It's worth a try, though."

"Well, this will cheer you up."

"What?"

"Ms. Cartwright, Jodie's social worker, called to tell me that Jodie has been asking for you. She said you would be allowed at least one supervised visit per day."

"I can see Jodie?" she asked, like it was too good to be true.

"Yes. Isn't that great news?"

"Really great news. Can I go today?"

"Sure. I'll take you right after work—that is if Ms. Cartwright can meet us there. How does that sound?"

"That sounds just fine," she answered, tears beginning to cloud her eyes. This time I could tell they were tears of joy.

I arranged for Ms. Cartwright to meet us at the hospital at four p.m. I certainly didn't want to tangle with that head nurse again. So, we agreed to meet in the main lobby. I encouraged Stella to bring Jodie a cookie from the café. Also, she still had the bag of toys to deliver. Stella hadn't seen Jodie for nearly a week. I was sure she would notice a big difference in her granddaughter's condition. As we boarded the elevator Stella seemed jittery. Her breathing sounded shallow and she was wringing her hands.

"Are you okay, Mrs. Leonard?" Ms. Cartwright asked.

"Yes, Ma'am… just excited to see Jodie. I'm so grateful to you, Ms. Cartwright. I been missin' my girl somethin' awful."

"Well, it's obvious she has been missing you, too. As I explained to you on the phone, I took the liberty of obtaining legal custody of Jodie for the state."

"Yes, Ma'am."

"How does that help Stella's case?" I asked.

"It will allow me to testify on her behalf. I'll need to arrange a few more supervised visitations, and a psych evaluation. Then, we can proceed with seeking custody."

"I see."

"In the meantime," Ms. Cartwright continued, now addressing Stella, "you'll be required to take parenting classes. Then, Jodie can be placed with you while the court sorts out her parents' situation."

"That sounds real good," Stella said. I was beaming at the prospect of Jodie and Stella being reunited.

When the elevator door opened, I was relieved to see no sign of Nurse Reynolds. Ms. Cartwright led us straight to Jodie's door and pushed it open carefully. The lights were dimmed, and Jodie—clutching her Teddy bear to her chest—was napping. I could tell that Stella was working hard to keep the tears at bay. Ms. Cartwright and I tiptoed around the beds to the opposite side of the room, next to the window, allowing Stella to enjoy a private reunion with her granddaughter. Stella approached slowly, rested her cane against the bedside cart, and leaned over the railing. Jodie stirred slightly and then stretched and yawned. She looked like a perfectly normal, well cared-for child. Her color was ever so much better than it had been when she first arrived. When she opened her eyes, she was looking in Stella's direction, but it seemed to take a moment or two for her eyes to focus—or perhaps she couldn't believe her grandmother had finally come. Suddenly, she sat up. She dropped her stuffed bear and reached for Stella, wailing in her husky, underused voice. "Stella!" she cried. "Stella, you came." They embraced for a long time and Stella's tears began to flow uncontrollably. Stella tried to hold the child at arm's length—to take a good look at her—but Jodie pulled her close again and wrapped her arms tightly around the woman's neck. "I was sad. I wanted Stella to come," she said.

"I missed you, too, Sweetie. I wanted to come. I'm here now."

"Don't cry, Stella." Now the child began talking like she had never been silent. Ms. Cartwright and I shared a look of amazement. "Hank is all gone," Jodie said. "Hank is in prison. Don't cry. Hank can't hurt us anymore." She was clutching her grandmother firmly as if she'd never let her go.

"Jodie, Sweetie, I'm so sorry Hank hurt my precious girl. Never again. He won't hurt us ever again. I love you, Sweetie." In awe, we watched the heartwarming scene as grandmother and granddaughter restored their obvious bond. Finally, Stella thought to offer a distraction in the form of toys. "Look here, Jodie. Edith—I—brought you something." A quick shake of my head reminded her of our previous agreement. Then, leaning against the radiator, Ms. Cartwright and I attempted to fade into the shadows.

"Child abuser, my eye," she said to me, quietly but adamantly. In that moment, I felt confident the case against Stella Leonard wouldn't hold sway with any reasonable judge. We watched for several minutes as Stella introduced one toy at a time showing Jodie how to play with each item.

"Shall we try the puzzle?" she asked, laying the pieces on Jodie's tray.

"I can walk," I heard the child exclaim at one point.

"That's wonderful, Jodie." Stella said. "After we finish this here puzzle you can show me, okay?"

"Okay." They seemed like any other grandmother and grandchild, talking, playing and enjoying each other's company. A casual observer would have never suspected that only two weeks before, both had been living in hell. Although no longer visible, the wounds were deep. It would take many years of therapy for them to heal.

We stayed in Jodie's room until an orderly brought her supper tray. I found the child's reaction both interesting and a little disturbing. Sweeping a mound of pink Play-Doh to the floor she reached greedily for the food and began shoveling it into her mouth with both hands. "Slow down, Baby,"

Stella said. "You'll choke."

"Jodie forgets," the child said, placing her hands resolutely in her lap. "Go slow. Use a spoon," she reminded herself and started the process anew. It was evident that either the nurses or the occupational therapist had been teaching the six-year-old how to eat like... well... like a human.

"Good girl. Much better," Stella praised. "Here's a cookie for later." She placed it on the tray next to the bowl of green Jell-O. "It tastes really good with milk."

"Cookie," Jodie repeated between spoons full of mashed potatoes.

"I need to go soon, Sweetie," Stella said when Jodie had nearly finished eating.

"No. Stella stay," Jodie pleaded. "Don't go. Stay with Jodie in the hospital."

"I'll come back tomorrow. I promise," said Stella. Jodie was becoming visibly anxious. "Finish your supper," Stella continued cheerfully. "Then you can show me how good you walk. Ms. Edith and Ms. Cartwright want to see you walk, too. Right?"

"Yes, Jodie," Ms. Cartwright chimed in, helping Stella keep the child distracted from her distress. "We want to see how well you walk. How many steps did you take yesterday?"

"Twelve steps with the walker and five all by myself."

"That's terrific, Jodie," I said. "You'll be running before long." After Jodie finished her supper, Stella helped her out of bed and the tiny girl demonstrated proudly her emerging skill. Just as she completed half of her dozen steps—counting each one aloud—Nurse Rebecca entered the room.

"You go, girl," she said. Then, addressing an enthusiastic audience of three, she asked, "Isn't she doing well?"

"Yes," we all agreed.

"Shall we walk your guests to the elevator, Jodie?" the nurse asked. "It's time for the playroom."

"That sounds like fun," Stella said. "I'll see you tomorrow, Sweetie." I could tell Stella was trying to sound positive so Jodie wouldn't become upset again.

"Don't go!" the child cried, reaching for her grandmother.

"Come on, give your grandmama a good-bye hug and I'll see you tomorrow," Stella said, kneeling in front of Jodie's walker with the help of her cane. They hugged and kissed like it was their last farewell, and Stella had to pry the girl's arms from around her neck.

Ms. Cartwright was holding the elevator door open, but it seemed that a major scene was about to accompany our exit. Fortunately, a quick-thinking

Rebecca saved the day. "Come on Jodie," she said. "Let's go ride the bouncy horse. Can you walk the whole way to the playroom today?" As the nurse diverted Jodie's attention toward the playroom we seized the opportunity to enter the elevator.

"Those pediatric nurses really know what they're doing," said Ms. Cartwright.

"They sure do." I agreed.

"Jodie looks real good," Stella said. "She's gonna be okay, ain't she—isn't she?" I smiled and nodded my approval of her correction.

"Yes, Mrs. Leonard. She's making excellent progress, and I can see how much she loves and needs you. I plan to talk to the judge and see if I can get the abuse charges against you dropped."

"You can do that?"

"I believe I can, but a couple of things must happen first."

"Like what?" The elevator door opened to the first-floor lobby and we stepped out.

"You will need to undergo a psychological evaluation, and you'll need to agree to take parenting classes."

"Anything." Stella said. "I'll do anything."

"You may still have to go before Judge Macintosh for the neglect charge, but he's a fair man. I'll be there to testify that you have shown yourself to be a loving guardian."

"Oh, thank you! Thank you, Ms. Cartwright. I'm beholden to you." As Stella vigorously shook the social worker's hand I was grinning from ear-to-ear.

"I like a happy ending as much as the next person," Ms. Cartwright replied. "But it's my responsibility to protect the children assigned to me. When I saw Jodie's condition, I naturally assumed you had neglected her intentionally and that you had been a participant in the abuse."

"I understand. I know how bad it looked. I was doin' the best I could to take care of Jodie and savin' my tip money to get us outta there—away from Hank."

Finally, Ms. Cartwright said, "Mrs. Leonard, the judge is going to ask why you didn't report your husband to the police."

"I reckon he will, at that. Well, before I went to Agape House and started them—those—sessions with Dr. Morgan, I couldn't have explained it. Now that I know about that battered wife thing it makes perfect sense to me. I guess you could say I didn't know I had a choice. It sounds crazy now, even to me, but back then I just felt trapped and ashamed. I was scared I'd lose Jodie just like I lost Amy."

"You don't need to be scared anymore, Stella," I said, as we bade good-bye to Ms. Cartwright and headed for the parking lot. "Now you have friends, a job and a place to live."

"And Jodie is safe. Don't forget the most important thing," she declared. "Jodie is safe."

Mike

I've got a lot on my plate these days with Amy's case and my exam coming up, but the thought of marrying Edith is keeping me energized. We don't have a date set for the wedding, and we haven't planned where we're going to live after we're married, but we're together now. That's what's important. We're together and we're committed to being together forever. I plan to make her the happiest woman alive. She sure has made me happy.

After breakfast at the café yesterday, Ted and I met with Amy's new attorney, Matthew Perkins. We were anxious to share the information about Grogan.

"Well, that changes everything," public defender Perkins said after hearing the news. "I'm going to appeal immediately. Can you bring Mr. Grogan to my office?"

"He may feel hesitant to leave his new job, but we'll see what we can do," Ted answered. "When do you want to see him?"

"As soon as possible. Tell him we'll reimburse him any lost wages. How about tomorrow morning at nine?"

"Mike, can you take care of that?" Ted asked.

"Of course," I assured him. I pulled a card from my wallet on which I had written the phone number of the service station. "I'll make the call as soon as we're finished here."

"And I need to see everything in the police report from Ms. Leonard's investigation," Perkins added. "Could I get the file this afternoon?"

"I'll bring it straight over," Ted said, as we turned to exit the defender's office.

"Oh, and one more thing," Perkins said. "I'll need to talk to Grogan's psychiatrist. What did you say his name was?"

"Southern," Ted said. "I don't know his first name, but Grogan said he works in the practice over on Ridgewood."

"Okay, I can look up the number. What about patient confidentiality? Will he be able to tell me anything?"

"Grogan said he'd instruct Dr. Southern to help us with the investigation. Maybe we can get him here at nine a.m., too."

"Perfect. Let's get this ball rolling and spring that poor girl from prison as soon as possible."

After arranging to pick up Grogan at the group home in the morning, I couldn't decide whom to call first with the good news, Edith or Stella. On second thought, maybe I shouldn't get their hopes up, in case things didn't work out in Amy's favor.

Chapter 20

Edith

Mike and I want to be married as soon as possible. We agree that we want to keep the wedding small and simple, but I've had enough experience with weddings to understand how challenging that goal might prove to be. I'll start by checking into available dates at the church.

I called my mom last night to tell her about our engagement. She sounded thrilled but wondered why I hadn't mentioned Mike before. I told her I was waiting until I could be sure Mike and I were committed to a long-term relationship. She adored Charlie. Because of that devotion, I knew she would have a hard time accepting another man in my life. I had to wait until I was sure.

Next, I called my brother, Winston. He said he was happy for me and promised that he and Meg and the girls would attend the wedding. As we were talking I could hear him sharing the news with Kristin and Kylie in the background—news which met with excited shrieks and unbridled chatter. When Winston asked the girls to leave the room so he could hear me, they insisted continuously upon talking to Auntie Edith until he was forced to relinquish the phone. "You're getting married? What's his name? Is he handsome like Uncle Charlie? When's the wedding? Oh, we'll need new dresses. And shoes. Have you decided on a color scheme yet? Can we help you pick out your gown? You will wear a wedding gown, won't you? Where will you hold the reception? Can we come early and help you get ready?" Comically, one question layered upon another until I couldn't answer properly any of them. Finally, Winston reclaimed the phone and sent his girls to their rooms with the promise that Auntie Edith would call back when the plans started in earnest and share every detail.

"Do you think they might be a little excited?" I asked, sarcastically, once we could hear each other again.

"Just a little," he said. "Meg will be thrilled, too. She's at a PTA meeting tonight. I'll let the girls share the news with her as soon as she gets home. Not that I could stop them if I wanted to." We both laughed and I promised to arrange a wedding planning visit with my nieces as soon as possible.

I had hoped to visit Amy to update her on the latest developments regarding both her mother and her daughter. As far as I knew she wasn't even aware Hank had been arrested. Also, I wanted her to know that Mike and Ted were making headway toward her possible release. Mike cautioned me not to raise her hopes, especially before Amy's new lawyer had spoken to her. I yearned to advocate for Stella. I thought Amy needed to know Stella had tried to protect Jodie from Hank… that she had been in a powerless situation. I wanted to tell her Jodie was safe now and getting good treatment.

Once again, Mike inserted the voice of reason. "Edith, you have such a big heart. You want everyone and everything to be okay. But, Sweetheart," (He had never used that term of endearment before,) "you're assuming responsibility that isn't yours to assume. Stella and Amy need to find their own way back to each other."

"I know you're right, but I feel so sad for them. They've been through hell through no fault of their own and I want…" Mike had not quite finished his breakfast of eggs, bacon, and grits, but he lowered his fork and took me by the hand. He led me back to my office. Once inside he closed the door and embraced me tenderly.

"Edith, I'm not telling you what to do, but it seems like your concern might be bordering on interference."

"I'm listening," I said into his chest. I was trying not to sound angry but I admit to feeling tingles of resentment creeping up my spine. As he released his embrace he led me to a chair and sat opposite me.

"One reason women get themselves into abusive relationships is dependence. They become so dependent on their abuser—both emotionally and financially—that they find themselves trapped. It's important for a battered woman to learn how to stand on her own."

"Are you saying my helping Stella is preventing her recovery?" I asked, with an edge to my voice.

"You've been a wonderful friend to Stella."

"But?" I interrupted, wondering if this conversation might escalate into our first argument.

"You can continue to be her friend and support her. I know you will because you care so deeply for other people. That's one of the things I love about you—your compassion. But you can't live Stella's life for her. You can't rescue her. If you do, it will take even longer for her to own her own power."

Whoa, Sergeant Travers! You're very good at this counseling stuff, I thought. As much as I didn't want to back down I had to admit Mike was right. I had nearly crossed a line, and my fiancé was both wise enough to recognize it and brave enough to bring it to my attention. I took a deep breath and let it out slowly. It gave me the time I needed to think straight.

"You're right," I said, reluctantly. "I'm a rescuer. I admit it and I know it's not emotionally healthy for either of us. I see someone suffering and I want to make it all better. I want to fix everything."

"I understand, Edith, but let's look at the facts. Ted and I are making good progress with the investigation. Amy's new lawyer seems hopeful and very competent. Stella's getting her feet on solid ground thanks to you and the shelter staff. From what you told me, Jodie's social worker is convinced Stella didn't abuse her and Ms. Fredrickson is working to get the charges dropped. So, you see, my darling," he concluded as he enfolded my hands in his and looked in my eyes, "you are doing—and have done—enough. Now you can step back and let the process unfold naturally."

"And let's not forget the best part," I added, yielding to his wisdom. "Hank Leonard is in prison where he'll likely stay for a long time."

"No, that's not the best news," he said, pulling me out of the chair and into his strong arms. He nibbled my ear and planted fervent kisses on my neck. His hands began moving tenderly up and down my torso until I thought I would cry out with desire.

"What's the best news?" I asked breathlessly, returning his probing kisses.

"Edith Bowman is going to be my wife. That's the best news." At that moment, I knew I was about to marry the most wonderful man in the whole world.

Mike

Edith and I have set a date for our wedding: September twelfth. To quote Edith, "It's only three short months away." Of course, if we did it my way, we'd go to the Justice of the Peace tomorrow, but my lovely fiancée informs me a three-month window is "bare-minimum planning time" for a church wedding. We spent a fair share of Saturday making decisions about invitations, color schemes, tuxedos, flowers, caterers, music, photography, wedding cakes, etc. After the first hour, I wanted to raise my hands and say, "Whatever you pick is fine with me," but I knew I would come across as cavalier. The truth is I don't care about such things, but Edith does. This so-called simple wedding is turning into a major shindig, especially since Edith's mother offered to spring for half the expenses.

In the meantime, my exam is looming with only a few days left to study. Ted has been firing questions at me every chance he gets. I feel like I'm well-prepared, but Mike Travers has been known to choke on tests.

Matthew Perkins, Amy's new attorney, doesn't let any grass grow under his feet. First, he read all the investigators' notes and newspaper articles from beginning to end. Then, after interviewing Robert Grogan and Grogan's psychiatrist, he petitioned the judge to order a competency hearing. The petition was granted. Next, he asked me to notify Amy that he is now representing her and that new evidence has come to light in her case. Immediately after I hand-delivered the notice to the prison, Perkins set up an appointment to meet with Amy. Finally, he petitioned the court for a new trial based on new evidence that could possibly overturn Amy's conviction. Perkins accomplished these tasks within the span of three days. He is convinced Amy received poor counsel from her original attorney who failed to establish Grogan as a viable witness. The man is a human dynamo. We should let him plan our wedding.

Stella

Ms. Fredrickson came to the café to tell me she scheduled a hearing with Judge Macintosh. She was actin' all excited. So, I guess that must be a good thing. She said I was to report to the courtroom on Monday morning at nine. "But I have to work," I said.

"Stella, when the judge tells you to come to court, you don't dispute it. You make it happen when he wants it to happen," she said. Edith heard us talkin' and came right over to where we was standin'.

"What does this mean, Ms. Fredrickson?" she asked.

"I'm hoping it means Stella won't have to stand trial."

"Do you think he'll drop the charges?"

"He said if Stella pleads guilty to the neglect charge, he can get the abuse charge dropped. Stella, I want you to bring someone from the shelter with you—someone who can testify that you were a victim of Battered Woman Syndrome. Do you have a peer counselor?"

"Yes, Ma'am, but I ain't—haven't—met her yet," I said.

"Okay, let me see if I can get Dr. Morgan to accompany you. I'll be there, of course, and Ms. Cartwright has been subpoenaed to testify, as well."

"So, is this meeting with the judge actually a trial?" Edith asked.

"Not exactly. It's a hearing to determine whether there's enough evidence against Stella to warrant a trial," she said. "It's called a probable cause hearing."

"May I attend?" Edith asked. "Stella will need me to drive her to the courthouse, anyway."

"It should be fine," Ms. Fredrickson answered.

"Thanks," Edith answered. Then to me she said, "Don't worry, Stella. I'll get someone to cover the breakfast shift for us."

I didn't sleep at all Sunday night. I was so nervous about seein' the judge. Edith said she'd come to the shelter at eight a.m. sharp. She told me I should wear my new dress and said she'd help me fix my hair. Well, I was up and waitin' for her way before she got there. I ate a few bites of breakfast. Then I took a shower and washed my hair. I was sittin' on my bed lookin' at some pictures of Amy and Jodie that I brought to the shelter in my duffle bag. There was a picture of Henry, too. I hadn't looked at it in years. Seein' my beautiful, dead boy was always too sorrowful. So, I kept the picture in a sealed envelope. But that mornin' I remembered somethin' Dr. Morgan told me. She said it's best to face our past hurts, not try to bury them. She said the pain will find its way to the surface one way or another. "If we face our sadness and talk about it," she told me, "the pain loses some of its power over us."

Dr. Morgan had got me to talk about most everything during our private sessions. I cried a lot and one time I even started screamin'. I couldn't help it. It was when I remembered Henry fallin' to his death. Dr. Morgan just let me scream and scream till I was all screamed out. Then she held me for a long time not sayin' anything, just holdin' me while I regurgitated the pain like bitter bile comin' up from a empty sick stomach. I didn't feel better right away, mainly cause I was embarrassed by my outburst, but the next mornin' I felt like somebody pulled me out from under a two-ton boulder.

While I was waitin' for Edith, I laid out them pictures on my bed all in a row, first Henry, then Amy and last was Jodie. For the first time, I could see how much they favored one another with their blonde curls and big, blue eyes. How could Hank bring himself to hurt them beautiful girls who looked so much like the boy he loved with all his heart? Then it struck me. When Hank beat Amy and Jodie (and me, too) he was flailin' against his heartbreakin' memories, tryin' to make them go away. Maybe if he hadn't got hooked on booze and dope he woulda' figured out it didn't help none. Just like he got addicted to drugs, he got hooked on violence. Like Dr. Morgan told me, understandin' ain't—isn't—the same as excusin', and forgivin' isn't the same as forgettin'. Right then I decided to forgive Hank, but I knew I couldn't never—no, that's a double negative—I couldn't ever let myself forget. It was my job to keep us safe—me and Amy and Jodie.

When Edith knocked on my bedroom door, I started to put them pictures away, but then I decided to show her. There was nothin' to hide anymore.

"Good, morning, Stella. Don't you look all spit-and-polished." she said. "What have you got there?"

"This here's my family," I said, proudly waving my hand over the gallery of snapshots.

"It certainly is. Look at Jodie. She looks so plump and healthy. Is this Henry?" she asked picking up the photo for a closer look.

"Yes, that's my sweet boy. Ain't he beautiful?"

"He is beautiful, Stella. How old was he in this picture, three or four maybe?"

"He just turned four. It's the last picture I took of him. I was waitin' till he got his kindygarten pictures from school."

"He looks so much like Jodie."

"I know. He does, don't he?" I agreed. Now I was cryin' and Edith was sittin' beside me, holdin' me and lettin' me mourn my beautiful dead Henry. But this time it felt different somehow. This time I didn't need to scream. Instead of seein' him plummeting to his death over and over, now I could remember my sweet boy laughing, running, and playing. I could remember his blue eyes sparklin' in the sunlight and his white curls bouncin' up and down like bed springs. This time I was able to stop my tears, knowin' there'd be more chances later to remember and to mourn. Like Dr. Morgan told me, the memories would never go away but now the deep pain could start to heal. I sat up, wiped my tears, and asked Edith if she would fix my hair.

"You bet," she answered, wiping her own tears. "Shall we put these on the dresser where you can look at them every day?" She was talkin' about my pictures. She lined them up in a row and I decided it was time to buy some frames.

My hair was still wet from the shower. I didn't own a hair dryer, but Edith come—came—prepared. She brought a tote bag with a hairdryer, curling iron, pins, comb and brush, and even scissors. "Would you mind if I trimmed it a little?" she asked. "I think it would look healthier if we cut off these split ends."

"You can't hurt it none, whatever you do. I ain't never—haven't n—ever—been good at fixin' hair."

"When I finish with you, you're going to wow that judge. Now, let's turn you away from the mirror. I want to surprise you." I felt a little nervous but I trusted Edith. Since she always looked like a model from a magazine, I figured she knew what she was doin'.

After about twenty minutes of cuttin', blowin', curlin' and combin' Edith declared me almost finished. "There's just one more thing," she said. "Let's brighten up those lips a little. Okay, give me a pucker like you just ate a lemon." I pursed my lips and she slathered on some pink lipstick. "You look beautiful. Are you ready to see the finished product?"

"I guess so," I answered, nervous-like. She spun me around and when I saw that woman in the mirror lookin' back at me I couldn't believe it was me—Stella Leonard. Edith had parted my hair to one side and cut it so it slanted to my chin. It was smooth and straight but the fat curling iron made the ends turn under just a tad. It made me look ten years younger—no, fifteen—especially with the lipstick that matched the pink in my dress. I looked away and when I turned back, for a spilt second I saw Amy. I always thought Amy was beautiful and here I was lookin' for all the world like my beautiful girl—except for the gray hair, that is. Hank told me again and again how ugly I was. Sometimes after we had sex he would say I was disgustin' or I made him sick to his stomach. I always believed him, but now I knew he was a liar.

I thanked Edith and hugged her. Even though I felt like a million bucks, I was embarrassed to leave the room and draw attention to myself. I still wasn't sure I deserved to feel so good. But Edith didn't give me a chance to wallow in self-pity.

"Come on, Stella," she said, taking my hand. "Let's go knock 'em dead."

When we got to the courthouse, I started feelin' real nervous again, but Edith kept encouragin' me and remindin' me the judge was just a person under that robe and all I had to do was tell the truth. "The truth will set you free," she said. She said she would stay right beside me and she'd be prayin' for me the whole time. That gave me courage.

Dr. Morgan and Ms. Cartwright met us at the courthouse, along with Ms.

Fredrickson. Together we climbed the long curving staircase to the second floor. It would've been easier on my hip to take the elevator but I suppose I was tryin' to delay the meetin'. I kept takin' deep breaths like Dr. Morgan said to whenever I got nervous. When we reached the landing, I turned to look at Edith. She gave me a big, confident smile and a thumbs-up.

At the big wooden doors of the courtroom, Ms. Fredrickson glanced at her watch and signaled the guard to open the door. I had never been in a real courtroom before, even for my bail hearing, but I had seen them on TV. It looked just like what I expected.

Ms. Fredrickson ushered us to the front row of seats and motioned for Edith to sit behind me. We waited just long enough for me to get real nervous. Then, in come the judge, wearin' a black robe. I was expectin' to see an old man with a long gray beard and them glasses you look over the top of, real threatnin'-like, but Judge Macintosh didn't look more than forty-five or so. His wavy hair was thick and brown. His brown eyes seemed kind. I don't know why his appearance set my mind at ease but it did… a little.

He was perched up high on his judge's bench, just like on TV. The bailiff said, "All rise for the honorable Judge Macintosh." We stood and then the bailiff said, "Be seated." Dr. Morgan was on one side of me and Ms. Fredrickson sat on the other side with Ms. Cartwright beside her. Across the aisle from us sat the district attorney. Next, Judge Macintosh told the bailiff to swear us in. The bailiff ordered us to stand again and swore us in making us promise to "tell the truth, the whole truth and nothing but the truth." I woulda told the truth anyway, but I guess that made it official. The judge read the charge against me and asked me if I understood.

"Yes, Sir," I answered.

"How do you plead, Mrs. Leonard, guilty or not guilty?" Ms. Fredrickson had advised me to plead guilty, but when I heard that word, "willfully" before the word "neglect" I couldn't do it.

"Judge Macintosh, Sir, can I talk to my lawyer for a minute?"

"What's going on here, Ms. Fredrickson?" the judge asked her. "I thought we agreed Mrs. Leonard would plead guilty to the neglect charge in exchange for the abuse charge being dropped."

"Yes, Judge, that was the agreement. May I have a moment with my client in private?"

"You may step outside, but don't take more than five minutes," he answered gruffly.

"Yes, Your Honor," she said, as she grabbed my cane and pulled me by the elbow toward the door. The district attorney followed us out.

"What are you doing, Stella?" Ms. Fredrickson asked when we reached the hallway. "I thought we agreed you would plead guilty. I explained that I'd stand a better chance of getting you a light sentence that way." I could tell she wanted to shout at me but she was tryin' hard to keep her voice down.

"I know, Ms. Fredrickson. I know what we agreed to but I can't plead guilty to bein' willful in neglectin' Jodie. It nearly killed me to see her suffer like that!" Suddenly I was shoutin' and I didn't care who heard me. "I didn't know I had a choice," I said. "I know it now but I didn't know it then. I swear I didn't. I just can't plead guilty when Hank is the guilty one. Please don't make me. It would be a lie and I promised to tell the truth." Edith musta heard me shoutin' from inside the courtroom because she come runnin' out the door like a bull was chasin' her.

"What is it? What's wrong?" she asked. Ms. Fredrickson threw up her hands, turned away, and walked to the stair railing as if to say, "I give up." The D.A. followed her and they stood talking like they was both mad.

"What's happened, Stella?" Edith asked, grabbing my shoulders.

"Oh, Edith! I can't plead guilty. She wants me to but I can't." I was gettin' a bit hysterical and people was starin' at us, but I didn't even try to calm down. This weren't… wasn't… a time to be calm. "I never wanted Jodie to get beat and starved half to death," I yelled. "I didn't want her to be chained to a bed in a dark room without a friend or a toy or even a blanket to keep her warm. I didn't want to neglect her. I wanted to be a lovin' grandmama. I wanted to talk to her and play with her and take care of her. You know that's the truth, don't you?"

"Of course, I do."

"You been tellin' me the truth will set me free. Do you still believe that?"

"Absolutely."

"Then I got to tell the truth." At this point, Ms. Fredrickson rejoined us. She seemed calmer now and looked resigned to lettin' me do what I needed to do.

"Okay, Stella," she said with a sigh. "I can't go against your wishes in this, but I also can't promise you won't go to prison."

"I understand," I said. Edith hugged me and then we all went back into the courtroom.

"Well, Ms. Fredrickson?" Judge Macintosh asked, soundin' kinda mean.

"With apologies, Your Honor, Mrs. Leonard wishes to change her plea."

"I see." he said. "This is highly irregular."

"Sorry, Your Honor," she answered sheepishly.

"Before I read the charge again, I'd like to hear from Ms. Cartwright and Dr. Morgan. Please remember you are under oath."

Ms. Cartwright told the judge about seein' me and Jodie together in the hospital and how much Jodie seemed to love me and need me and how she, Ms. Cartwright, that is, was convinced I never hurt the child. "In fact," she said, "despite my initial assumptions, I'm convinced Mrs. Leonard actually saved the child's life more than once. Further, Your Honor, Mrs. Leonard has willingly submitted to—and passed—a psych evaluation and has agreed to take parenting classes."

When it was Dr. Morgan's turn to talk, she described Battered Woman Syndrome and said how Hank was beatin' me every day and controllin' me with his words and his violence until I was too afraid to stand up to him or call the police… how I was afraid Jodie would be taken away if I called the police. Then Ms. Fredrickson pulled out them pictures that Jessica took when I first come to the shelter. I had forgot about 'em. She asked permission to show them to the judge and he said, "Permission granted."

"May I?" asked the D.A. and the judge motioned for him to step forward. The judge spread them pictures out on his desk. The two of them stared for a long time, and I started feelin' embarrassed cause I knew they was lookin' at my near-naked body. Then the D.A. returned to his seat. Finally, the judge looked up with a blank expression and took a deep breath. I tried to read his face but I couldn't.

"Would both attorneys please approach the bench?" he said at last. The three of them talked for a while. We couldn't hear what they was sayin' and I was getting more nervous by the minute. Finally, the two lawyers came back to their seats.

"Mrs. Leonard, please stand," the judge said at last. I stood on shaky legs held up by my cane on one side and my lawyer on the other. I held my head high, knowin' I had told the honest truth."

"Mrs. Leonard, I have read the documents and viewed the photographs submitted in your defense. I have heard statements from two qualified experts. Additionally, the district attorney has informed me that—" He cleared his throat, "—your tirade in the hallway, while it cannot be entered into record, has helped to convince him of your innocence. He has dropped all charges against you. Therefore, the court finds that there is no substantial reason to warrant a criminal trial. You are free to go."

As the room erupted in shrieks and applause, my wobbly legs failed me and I plopped down in stunned silence. I couldn't believe what I heard. Could it be true? The other women were huggin' and squealin' with delight so I guessed it must be good news.

"Stella, you're free. The judge said you're free." Now Edith was pulling me up outta my chair and huggin' me. That's when it hit me. I was free... free to start my life over again, free to love and care for my granddaughter till her own mama gets outta prison. It was a miracle.

Chapter 21

Edith

I've never been one to bite my fingernails, but that hour spent at the courthouse was stressful enough to cause even me to sacrifice a perfectly good manicure. When I heard Stella yelling at the top of her lungs outside the courtroom, I thought she had just learned she was going to prison. Poor Dolly. The woman looked like she was working herself up to a heart attack. After the judge announced that Stella was free, cheering erupted. For a moment, Stella looked dazed and confused, but once the reality of Judge Macintosh's words hit her, she became more animated than I have ever seen her—other than her scene in the corridor, that is. She was shaking hands, hugging and saying, "thank you" to everyone in the courtroom, including the stenographer and the bailiff.

As we drove to the café, Stella and I reviewed the whole hearing so I could relate it to Mike later. It was wonderful to see her so deliriously happy for a change. We had finished in plenty of time before the lunch rush so I took a quick detour. When I pulled the car up to the curb in front of my church, Stella looked puzzled. "What are we doing here?" she asked.

"There's one more person we need to thank," I said. I was glad to find the front door unlocked and the sanctuary empty. Hand-in-hand, we walked down the center aisle and knelt at the altar. "I prayed the whole time we were in the courtroom," I told Stella, "and now it's time to say 'thank you.'"

"Was you prayin' for a miracle?" Stella whispered.

"No. I prayed that whatever happened in there, God would be with you and give you strength. It was God's idea to grant your miracle."

Mike

Edith called last night to share the wonderful news about Stella. I've seen many domestic abuse hearings go the other way. So, I was preparing for the worst. I fully expected Stella would have to serve some jail time, and I knew such a result would devastate Edith. Now that the hearing is over, Ted and I can focus on getting Amy released from prison and bringing this family back together.

Edith said that, while I'm taking my exam Saturday, she and Stella will be shopping for wedding gowns. "If I don't have something totally distracting to keep my mind occupied," she said, "I'll worry myself to death about your exam."

"It sounds like you don't have much confidence in your fiancé," I said, playfully.

"Of course I do. It's just that I know how important this promotion is to you and I want you to do well."

"I was teasing you, Edith. Now you and Stella have fun shopping, and I'll call you as soon as I'm finished, okay?"

"Okay. Go get 'em, Mike. I love you."

"I love you, too."

In the meantime, Grogan's competency hearing was set for the following Wednesday. Matthew Perkins—who completed his investigation in record time—arranged for me to accompany him to the prison. He thought Amy might be less intimidated by him if she saw a familiar face. The interview has been arranged for early next week.

Perkins explained that his strategy is to convince a new judge to declare a mistrial. According to him, this decision needs to happen before Amy's next parole hearing. Otherwise she might be granted parole instead of pardon. Perkins is determined to petition for a full pardon. He feels confident he can get Amy fully exonerated, which means she'll be released without a criminal record to haunt her the rest of her life.

With everything going on in both of our lives, Edith and I haven't been alone together since the night I proposed. Is this how it's going to be? Now that we're engaged do we spend less time together instead of more? Of course, my sensible side understands the situation is temporary, but my romantic side longs to spend every possible minute with the woman I love.

I hope I wasn't too hard on her about her relationship with Stella. Edith is so caring. She feels everybody's pain. Her compassion is one of the things I love about her, but she needs to let Stella find her own way to self-confidence and independence. From what I've learned as a cop, excessive outside help can delay that important process.

Chapter 22

Edith

There's a little bridal shop just down the street from my café. I've passed it often, but I've never gone inside. Mind you, I'm not looking for anything white and fluffy. This is not my first wedding after all. I'm not a twenty-year-old blushing bride who wants to look like a princess.

Right after the breakfast shift Saturday morning, I walked to the shop and spent a couple of hours browsing through the merchandise. Stella took the bus and met me after her session with Dr. Morgan. As I tried on at least a dozen gowns of various cuts and styles, Stella gushed over each one, in turn, but I couldn't get excited about any of them. Soon it became clear that my vision wouldn't be realized in this shop. However, I found a perfect bridesmaid gown in a lovely shade of teal—just what I had in mind. I insisted Stella model it for me. Except for the length, it fit her perfectly and looked stunning on her. "We'll take it," I told the consultant who likely had given up making a sale at that point.

"It sure is purty, but how do you know it'll fit your bridesmaid?" Stella inquired.

"It fits you doesn't it?"

"But, don't she need to try it on to be sure?"

"Stella, I want you to be my attendant. That is if you agree, of course."

"Really? Me? Are you sure?"

"I didn't want to ask until I knew… well… until I was certain you wouldn't be in prison, but I'm asking now. Stella, will you be my maid (or rather, matron) of honor?"

"I ain't—haven't—ever done it before. I don't know what to do but it'll be a real honor. Yes, I will."

"Thank you. Do you like the dress?"

"I love it. I have—not—haven't ever…" (I could tell she was choosing her words carefully to avoid a double negative.) "…haven't ever had a beautiful dress like this, not even for my own wedding. I wore my best Sunday dress—which Mama made a few years before—but it was real plain. I didn't have flowers or a veil or nothin'… not even a ring. We just drove to the next town and got married at the courthouse. Then we moved into Ms. Flannery's place."

"What about a honeymoon?" I asked, feeling sad.

"Hank took me to supper at the motor court restaurant."

"That was it?"

"That was it," she said. I wanted to cry, but it seemed like Stella and I had shed enough tears lately to float a battleship. Instead I changed the subject.

"I hope Mike is doing well on his exam. He sounded pretty nervous last night."

"Oh, I'm sure the sergeant—"

"Soon to be lieutenant," I interrupted, proudly.

"Yeah, I'm sure Lieutenant Travers will do just fine. He's real smart." By the time we headed back to the café we were making plans to check out some stores at the mall the following week.

"Did Mike tell you he and Matthew Perkins are going to see Amy next week?" I asked, as we entered the café.

"No. I ain't—haven't—talked to him much lately. Does that Perkins feller think he can get my Amy outta that place?"

"He seems confident he can get her conviction overturned."

"What does that mean?"

"It means your daughter might be coming home soon."

"Well, then, I best make sure she has a proper home to come to."

Chapter 23

Stella

Edith asked me to be her matron of honor. I couldn't believe it. She had me tryin' on these beautiful gowns, one after the other, but I never suspected she was gonna ask me. I hope I don't embarrass her. I ain't never been a bridesmaid before. In fact, I ain't—haven't—even been to a church weddin' in my whole life. I'm excited but nervous, too. What if I mess up or trip over my cane or somethin'?

Edith said Amy might be gettin' outta prison soon. I was thrilled to hear it but it got me thinkin' about where she would go. We can't go back to that awful place where me and Jodie and Hank was livin'. It ain't fit for humans, especially with all them bad memories. Tomorrow I'll call that sorry landlord and tell him we're movin' out. The rent's paid till the end of the month, so I can get in to take what little belongs to me. Hank's stuff can rot for all I care.

I got till September at the shelter. When Jodie gets outta the hospital she can come live with me there. Then maybe I'll get some of that welfare money to help till I'm on my feet. Dr. Morgan keeps tellin' me I'm gettin' stronger and more independent. She says I should be proud of my progress. I know she's right but I still feel scared a lot. I'm just happy I don't have to go to prison and Jodie didn't get took away.

Last night at "group" Ruth started talkin' about her husband. She said she finally got up the nerve to leave him after nine years of marriage and a whole lot of beatin's. She has two teenage kids from her first marriage who live with their father. She decided they was better off bein' raised by a cheater than watchin' her get beat up every day. So, she gave up custody.

Dr. Morgan asked her what finally made her call the shelter. "It was my weekend with my kids," Ruth said. "The kids and I were planning to go out for breakfast and then school shopping. They were still asleep and Martin was getting dressed to meet a client. Martin liked to have his dress shirts ironed and folded just so. I had spent a good part of Friday ironing nearly a dozen shirts and as many pairs of trousers. I had carefully folded each shirt just the way he liked them and placed them in his wardrobe in neat piles. I was in the bathroom brushing my teeth when I heard him yell, 'God damn it!' I opened the door and saw all of those carefully ironed and folded shirts on the floor in a heap. I guess he had tried to pull from the middle causing the whole pile to topple. I rushed to his aid as was my usual pathetic behavior and started picking up the shirts and reassuring him it was no problem."

"'It's okay,' I said. 'I'll take care of it.' I knew, from past experience, what was about to happen, and I didn't want him to wake the kids and expose them to his ranting.

"I was on my hands and knees refolding and piling his shirts neatly when he grabbed my arm and jerked it behind me with such force I heard a loud crack, and I could feel a separation at my shoulder. The pain was excruciating. He was screaming at me, 'Can't you do anything right? You know I have an appointment at eight o'clock and now I'm going to be late! You are the sorriest excuse for a wife! No wonder Jerry divorced you!' He said plenty more too, but I was writhing in pain on the floor and still trying to soothe his temper."

"I think we can guess what happened next," Dr. Morgan said, "but please continue." Julia was starting to cry, and Samantha looked like she wanted to kill somebody. Tressa was staring at the floor and nodding slowly as if to say I've been exactly where you've been. I felt sick to my stomach.

"One after the other, Martin feverishly unfolded the shirts that I had ironed so painstakingly and started tossing or kicking them at me. Just then Jerry my fourteen-year-old came to the door. When he saw me on the floor he rushed forward to help me. That's when Martin grabbed my son by the hair, pulled him up, and pushed him into the door jamb. 'Get out of here,' he yelled. 'This is none of your damn business.' Jerry was stunned momentarily which gave Martin a chance to kick me in the face breaking my cheekbone."

"As I was losing consciousness, I heard my thirteen-year-old daughter screaming, 'Stop! You're killing her.'"

"I came to in an ambulance in unbearable pain. I remained conscious just long enough to hear Martin telling a police officer about my 'accident.' As my world faded to black again, I knew he would get away with his lies and abuse like he always had but—worse than that—I knew I would never see my kids again."

"I was in the hospital for three weeks. I had to have one surgery to repair my shoulder and another to repair my eye socket. The ophthalmologist couldn't guarantee I would regain my sight. Fortunately, most of it has returned."

"Did you file charges?" Dr. Morgan asked.

"Not at first. I was so depressed and defeated. I just wanted to die. No one except Martin came to see me in the hospital. It turns out he hadn't even called my parents. Of course, Jerry wouldn't let the kids anywhere near me."

"Oh, Ruth, how horrible," said Samantha. The rest of us were pretty much stunned into silence.

Finally, Dr. Morgan said, "Let me guess. Martin was repentant and solicitous while you were hospitalized."

"Oh, yes," said Ruth. "He sat by my bed day after day and cried. Most of the time I pretended to be asleep."

"'It'll never happen again,' he said. 'I love you so much, Ruthie. You're the love of my life. I promise to take care of you.' It was nauseating. One time I heard two nurses talking. Martin had just left and they thought I was asleep.

"'Her poor husband. He's so devoted to her. He seems devastated.'

"I know. Yesterday I found him crying. When I assured him she would recover, he said, 'I just love her so much'."

"That lying, deceitful bastard," Julia said.

"Actually, Julia, he probably was remorseful," said Dr. Morgan, "but did that mean the abuse would stop?"

"Hell, no!" Tressa said, standing and starting to pace. "They never stop. They just keep beatin' on us till they kill us or somebody stops 'em."

"Please have a seat, Tressa," the doctor said. "We're almost out of time. Let's save your story for tomorrow evening."

"Yeah, okay. Sorry." Tressa sat down but she was too worked up to sit still.

"You may have the entire hour if you need it. All right, Tressa?"

"Yeah. Fine. I just get so furious."

"Everyone here understands," Dr. Morgan said, "and it's good to let yourself feel those feelings." Ruth stood and walked to where Tressa was seated and placed her good arm around the disturbed woman's shoulders.

"I'm okay now, and you will be, too," Ruth said. That's when I realized we was becomin' a family. Black, white, rich, poor, young or old, it didn't make no difference. It didn't make any difference. We was sisters, united by our common condition. Together, with Dr. Morgan's help, we could lift ourselves and each other out of our circumstances and start new lives filled with hope.

Edith

I had just stepped out of the shower and was pouring my second cup of coffee when I heard somebody pounding on my door. My first thought was the building was on fire and I'd have to evacuate with wet hair and no make-up, wearing nothing but a towel. When I looked through the peephole I saw Mike standing in the hallway looking frantic. He was shifting from one foot to the other like a little boy who desperately needed to pee.

"Mike, what on earth? What's wrong?" I asked as I opened the door. "Is it the exam? Did you pass your exam?"

"No... I mean I don't know yet. It's Amy."

"Amy? What about Amy? Is she all right? Did you see her?"

"Yes, no... You're not going to believe..." Excitedly, he was twirling his hat in his hands as I tried to usher him toward a chair. "I can't stay, but I had to come and tell you in person. Amy's being released today."

"What? Today? How?" I was incredulous.

"It was that lawyer, Perkins. He got the judge to overturn her conviction."

"So fast? Wow! Mike that's amazing!"

"Listen, I have to get going, but somebody needs to break the news to Stella. I knew you'd want to be the one to do it."

"Absolutely. I'll call her right away."

"They're releasing Amy at noon. Can you drive Stella to Hendersonville? I can't get away today."

"Of course. I'll have to call in some forces to cover the restaurant but I wouldn't miss this reunion. Will you be in for breakfast?"

"No. That's why I stopped by. I have to go to court this morning."

"Oh, I thought you just wanted to see me wearing nothing but a towel," I teased.

"That's definitely a bonus," he said, wrapping his arms around me and nibbling my neck. "Mm, you smell even better than you look."

"I wish you could stay," I said, letting my towel drop to the floor.

"Me, too. Oh, me too."

As Mike's strong hands caressed my backside, we kissed longingly. Then, gently removing my hungry arms, he pushed me away, took a long, lustful look at my naked form and sighed deeply.

"Wow," he said. "That image should hold me for a couple of hours." He shook his head, as if to wake himself from a trance, put on his hat and headed for the door. "Call me when you get back, okay? Love you."

"I will. I love you too. Bye." I couldn't wait to call Stella, but first I had to see if Melinda and Sam could cover the café without Edith and me. Melinda sometimes enlisted her teenage daughter to wait tables. I was hoping the girl would be available.

"Stella, put on your dress and fix your hair like I showed you," I said without preamble. "I'm picking you up at ten thirty, no, ten o'clock."

"What? Why? What about work?" she asked.

"Forget about work today. You're not going to believe this."

"Believe what?"

"Amy's being released from prison today, and we're going to Hendersonville to pick her up." My announcement was met with silence.

"Stella, are you there? Did you hear what I said?"

"I heard it, but I can't believe it. Are you sure? My Amy's comin' home?"

"That crackerjack lawyer of hers got her conviction overturned."

"Oh, Edith. You were right. You said not to give up hope. You said to believe in the system and believe in God and you were right. I just can't believe... oh, my! My baby's comin' home."

I dressed hurriedly and gobbled a handful of dry cereal. It was still early, but nervous energy about the impending reunion caused my adrenalin to flow. I knew Amy would need some street clothes and I wanted to make sure there was time to stop by the mall.

Just as I grabbed my purse and headed for the door, my cell phone rang. It was Stella.

"Edith, what am I gonna' do about Jodie? I can't let Amy see her in the hospital. I thought I'd have more time."

"Don't worry, Stella. We'll figure out everything. It'll be fine," I said. "I'm on my way."

When I arrived at the shelter, I headed straight to Wendy's office. At the risk of Mike's disapproval, I needed to make sure Amy had a place to stay, starting tonight. And then there was Jodie. She would be coming home soon, too. Wendy assured me Amy could take the other bed in Stella's room until Jodie was released from the hospital. Then, the three of them would have to move to the other building, she said.

With that settled, I started bounding up the stairs. Halfway up I spotted Stella at the top of the flight. She looked amazing. She had done a great job with her hair and was wearing lipstick and a bit of blush.

"Stella, you look beautiful," I said, stopping in my tracks.

"So, you think Amy will like it?" she asked, fanning her skirt.

"Absolutely. Come on, let's get going."

"What's the rush?" she asked as we descended the stairs. "It only takes half an hour to get to Hendersonville." I explained that we were going shopping first.

Already, I dreaded getting my credit card bill for the month, but I couldn't let Amy show up at Agape wearing an orange jumpsuit with "Women's Correctional Facility" printed across the back. We picked out a pair of jeans in size four and another in size six just in case. Then we added a couple of t-shirts, two sundresses marked down to half price, and a sweater. Next, we headed to the shoe department where we grabbed a pair of size-six sandals and some runners. Although Amy had appeared very thin to Stella, she figured her daughter's shoe size probably hadn't changed. The young woman would need a whole wardrobe, but at least these initial purchases would get her started in her new civilian life.

We were not prepared for the scene that awaited us outside the prison. Nearly a dozen cops had been enlisted to contain the swarm of news reporters and photographers converging at the entrance. The media didn't miss an opportunity for a story, and this story must be a big one, we surmised. Not only was Hendersonville's media represented thoroughly, but we saw news trucks from every surrounding town, including our own. Since I couldn't find a parking place close to the entrance, I decided to drop off Stella and proceed to the overflow lot. Of course, a policeman stopped us and asked for identification. "What's going on?" I asked after rolling down my window.

"You can't stop here," he said. "Amy Leonard is being released at noon."

"All of this is for Amy?"

"Yeah, it's big news. Her conviction has been overturned and she's free to go."

"I know that. This is her mother," I said motioning to Stella.

"We're here to take her home, and this woman is disabled."

"Oh, I see. Can you provide some form of identification, Mrs. Leonard?" He was leaning down peering through my open window. I could smell stale garlic on his breath.

"I don't have a driver's license, Sir," Stella answered, working to be heard over the din. "What about my social security card? Will that do?"

"Yes, that should be fine." He checked the card that she pulled from her wallet with shaky hands and handed it back through the window. "Okay, Ma'am, let her out here." Then, he stood and shouted to a fellow officer over the roof of my car. "Hey, Jones, come over here and keep an eye on this lady. Keep the reporters away until her friend comes back."

Officer Jones helped Stella out of the passenger side, and I heard someone shout, "That's Leonard's mother." As the questions started flying, one after the other, microphones and cameras leaned forward, and the cops had to physically restrain the reporters. Stella looked frightened, making me hesitate to leave her even long enough to park the car.

"Don't worry ma'am. She'll be fine till you get back." Two officers walked Stella closer to the building and stood between her and the mob.

"I'll be right back Stella," I called. As I pulled away from the entrance, a group of reporters gathered around my car and followed me, firing questions from every direction. Quickly I rolled up my window, locked the doors, and tried to carefully maneuver my car through the crowd. I wondered how I would make it back to Stella without being trampled. Just then a cop knocked on the passenger-side window motioning for me to let him in. I unlocked the door and he jumped in.

"Park over there," he instructed. "I'll walk you back."

"This is crazy," I said. "Can't these people find something more newsworthy to cover, like a murder or a bank robbery? Amy will freak when she sees this."

"In a town the size of Hendersonville, anything bigger than a lost pet is newsworthy."

"How will I get Amy and Stella to my car without being trampled?"

"Don't worry. We'll place the three of you in my cruiser and drive you out here. Then I'll block the main exit until you're out of sight."

"Thank you. I really appreciate your help." As I took the farthest parking space from the prison entrance, I proceeded to tell Chris—that was his name—that I was engaged to a cop. During our considerable walk back to the prison we had a nice chat about his wife and kids until, once again, the throng of reporters engulfed us.

"Just keep walking," Chris said as he took me by the arm. "You aren't obligated to answer any questions." I held on to his arm like my life depended on it.

"Is that gun loaded or do I need to remember my karate moves?" I quipped, trying to keep my nerves under control.

"Don't you worry, ma'am. I've got you covered." I thought about Mike and hoped he had passed his lieutenant's exam. The sooner he got off the beat the safer he would be.

The clock on the tower in front of us read eleven fifty-five. Those five minutes until noon would be some of the longest of Amy's and Stella's lives. The time would stretch for me, too. I wondered how much disorder might erupt when the clock struck twelve. Fortunately, the police force seemed prepared to handle any situation.

When I reached Stella, she relaxed into my arms. "I'm so nervous," she said.

"Don't worry," I said. "The cops have everything under control."

"It's not just the crowd and the questions. I'm worried Amy won't be glad to see me. What if she doesn't want to come?" Just then a sergeant approached.

"Okay, ladies. Here's the plan. Amy will be escorted by her attorney and a female guard. Mr. Perkins is prepared to give a brief statement to the press. Then he'll answer a few questions."

"Will Amy have to say anything?" Stella asked.

"We're leaving that up to her and her lawyer," he said. "As soon as Perkins gives us the signal, that cruiser over there will pull right up to the door, blocking the entrance. I want you two to hop in the back. Amy will sit in the front. You'll be driven to your car and allowed to leave the premises with another cruiser right behind you. We'll block the main exit for ten minutes, giving you a head start."

"Do you think they'll follow us?" I asked.

"It's likely, so don't dawdle."

"Here she comes," someone shouted. "It's Amy Leonard." The noise rose to an ear-shattering level and Stella grabbed my arm.

"It's her. My baby is free," she said. As Amy and Matthew Perkins walked toward us, Stella began shaking all over.

"May we?" I asked the officer, motioning toward Amy.

"Yes. Go ahead." The moment Amy and Stella spotted each other, the cacophonic noise seemed to fade to silence. I heard nothing except the cries of a mother and daughter being joyfully reunited. I stood back as they fell into each other's arms. We were surrounded protectively by policemen and guards, who ensured the reunion received the decorum it deserved. Perkins approached a make-shift podium just in front of the prison to speak into the jumble of microphones that were attached. As he pulled a piece of paper from his breast pocket and unfolded it, a hush fell over the crowd.

"Ladies and Gentlemen of the press. Today marks an auspicious occasion in the halls of justice—a day that should make every one of us both ashamed and proud to be an American. After three long years of imprisonment for a crime she was forced to commit under threat of bodily harm or death, Amy Leonard is a free citizen. Her criminal record has been expunged by the Honorable Judge Gregory Tanner.

"For three years, Amy Leonard has been a victim of incompetent legal representation and unjust imprisonment. She has suffered untold physical and mental anguish both in prison and outside its walls, but she has survived and overcome. In the end, she has been victorious and today she walks away, not only a free woman but an educated citizen. Yes, Ms. Leonard served three years behind bars, but during that time she took advantage of the opportunity to earn a degree. She knew the importance of looking to the future and never giving up. She worked hard to make sure that once she completed her unjustified sentence she would be prepared to return to society as a responsible contributing member. That's right. A few weeks ago, Ms. Leonard accepted her college diploma signifying a degree which she earned in three years instead of the usual four."

Now the group exploded with applause and shouts of "Congratulations, Amy!" "Well done!" "You're my hero, Amy Leonard!" Amidst the kudos, an alert cop summarily led one, but only one, heckler away to a squad car.

"Now, I'm sure you have questions for me and for Ms. Leonard," Perkins continued. "We will answer what we can for the next five minutes. After that I implore you to respect Ms. Leonard's privacy as she acclimates to her new life." Immediately the reporters began firing questions. Matthew Perkins, seeming far more poised than his years of experience could have afforded him, answered each one in turn. Finally, he motioned for Amy to join him at the podium. More applause greeted her. She looked so very young and frail, but at least she was no longer wearing that awful orange jumpsuit. A blush crept up her neck and turned her pale face bright pink. Her striking blue eyes betrayed an underlying sadness.

"How does it feel to be a free woman, Amy?" asked one female reporter.

Amy paused, looked out over the crowd, took a deep breath, and cleared her throat. Her shaky voice began quietly then increased in volume. "I hope... I hope none of you ever has to go through what I have experienced in order to appreciate your freedom. After three long years of imprisonment, today I feel like I have been resurrected from the dead."

"Where will you live?"

"I don't know yet."

"When will you be reunited with your daughter, Ms. Leonard?"

"As soon as possible, I hope."

"How is she? Is it true that she has been locked in a room and abused for three years?"

"Where is she? When will you see her?" Perkins shook his head as if to say, "Don't answer that."

"No comment."

"What will you do now?"

"Now I will try to live as normal a life as possible and provide that for my daughter."

Perkins stepped in front of Amy and signaled the sergeant to facilitate our exit. "Thank you, ladies and gentlemen," he said into the microphones. "This concludes the press conference." Per the prearranged plan, he escorted Amy to the squad car that had pulled up to the entrance right on cue. I took Stella's elbow, helped her climb into the backseat, and followed her. Amy took the front passenger seat. Within seconds we were speeding toward my car and our escape.

The officer helped Amy and Stella into the back seat, and I locked the doors. All the way back to town Amy and Stella talked non-stop. Amy seemed liberated from any malice she had felt previously toward her mother. At one point, I overheard Stella explaining Jodie's situation bravely to her daughter. Sharing the whole sordid truth about Jodie's abuse would risk the only thing that mattered to Stella—her relationships with her daughter and her grand-daughter. It took great courage but she did it. She told Amy everything. They held each other and cried over Jodie's lost childhood. Together, they pledged to make up for the years of neglect and abuse.

"When can I see her?" Amy asked.

"Let's get you settled in the shelter," I interjected. "Tomorrow we'll make arrangements for you to visit Jodie in the hospital."

"Oh, I almost forgot," said Stella. "We brought you some clothes. Would you like to change out of them old ratty clothes before we get home? They don't do nothin' for your purty... pretty blue eyes. Oops! I meant to say they don't do...anything...for...your...pretty, blue eyes. How was that, my smart ed-ucated daughter?" The three of us shared a much-needed laugh at Stella's deliberate self-corrections. For a moment, I felt a twinge of jealousy. Would I ever talk and laugh with a daughter? Or a son for that matter?

Stella

Headin' over to Hendersonville to pick up Amy was one of the scariest things I ever done. As much as I wanted to see my girl and wrap my arms around her—as much as I wanted her to get outta that prison for good—I didn't know if she would still be holdin' a grudge. She had a right to. That's for sure.

But I was becomin' a different person now that Hank was outta my life. Dr. Morgan—and Edith, too—been showin' me I'm worth somethin' and now I'm startin' to get me some self-respect. Hank beat every bit of that outta me, I guess, but now I knew it weren't—it wasn't—too late to get it back.

Ms. Cartwright said that Amy and I would need to take parenting classes, and that our visits had to be supervised a couple more times, but then we could take Jodie home and be a real family.

Anyway, when Amy started runnin' toward me, callin' "Mama," and collapsed in my arms, I knew everything was gonna be okay. As we were drivin' away from that hideous building that had kept my beautiful, innocent daughter locked up for three years, I wouldn't let myself look back. It was our chance—Amy's and mine—to start life again. I only wanted to look forward.

In the car, Amy changed outta them ugly clothes. She looked so thin. She put on them size four jeans and one of them shirts Edith bought her. I stuffed the horrid rags in a bag, and when we got to the shelter, I carried it around to the side and threw it in the dumpster.

Everybody was waitin' for us: Ruth, Samantha, Tressa, Julia, even Wendy and Dr. Morgan and some women from the other house. And the cook, Madelyn, was there too. They had been watchin' TV and saw us on the breakin' news report. When we came through the front door they started clappin' and huggin' us like we were long-lost family or somethin'. I could tell Amy felt real uncomfortable with all them strangers huggin' her, but I held her hand and quick asked everybody to sit down in the front room. Then I started makin' the introductions. I couldn't believe how sweet and welcomin' they all were to my girl. Nobody asked the questions that surely musta been on their minds. They just said things like, "I'm glad to meet you" and "Welcome to Agape House," and stuff like that. I guess they figured Amy done answered enough questions for one day.

After a few minutes, Wendy said, "Amy, you must be worn out from all the excitement. Ladies, let's let Stella get her daughter settled in their room. We'll see them again at dinner." I felt so relieved and I could tell Amy did too. We said "thank you" and walked Edith to the door.

"I'll see you in the morning, Stella," Edith said. Then Edith held Amy's shoulders and looked her straight in the eyes like Edith always did with people. "Amy, I'm so happy for you," she said, and I knew she meant it.

"I can't thank you enough for all you done to help us, Edith," I said, giving her a big hug.

"Hey, that's what friends do, remember? They help each other."

"Yeah, but the helpin' has been all one-sided so far."

"Oh, you just wait till your matron-of-honor duties start in earnest," she said. Then she hugged me and hugged Amy one more time. "Bye, Amy. Congratulations!"

Amy and me—Amy and I—climbed the stairs to our room, and after she took a long, hot shower, we both slept till suppertime. I slept right through my dinin' room duty and nobody woke me.

Mike

I did it. I passed my exam. In fact, I aced it. I could hardly wait to tell Edith. I was now—or soon would be—a lieutenant in charge of my own department. Granted, my department would consist of only two other officers, but still, my own department. While the increased paperwork didn't appeal to me, the increase in salary certainly did. Ten thousand dollars a year added to my salary plus bonuses would ensure that I could provide Edith a stable financial future. She could even sell the café if she decided to. Other than her restaurant, neither of us had any equity, but we could save the rent money from my studio apartment by sharing hers for a couple of years. Then maybe we can afford to buy a house and start a family. But, I'm getting ahead of myself. "Counting my chickens before they hatch," like my dad used to say. Wouldn't he be proud? It had always been his dream for me to follow in his footsteps and now I was on my way. I wish he were alive to see me get my promotion.

As usual, I headed over to the café for dinner, fit to burst. I could have called Edith with the news but I wanted to tell her in person. Of course, Edith would have big news to share with me too. I had been in the courtroom since eight o'clock that morning and hadn't listened to the radio or seen a TV screen all day. I was anxious to hear about Amy's release, but I knew if I didn't make my announcement first I wouldn't be a very good listener.

I had an idea. I stopped by the Rite Aid on Highway 127 where I picked up some white poster board and markers. I laid the sheet of cardboard on the hood of my cruiser and pulled the markers from the bag. Now, I never claimed to be an artist, but my rendering of an eight-point lieutenant's cap--complete with gold braid and insignia—wasn't half bad. Of course, the gold was actually yellow but it served the purpose. Below the cap, I scrawled the words, "Call me LIEUTENANT Mike now."

My sign elicited the exact reaction I had hoped it would. When Edith saw it, she started jumping up and down and screeching like a five-year-old girl on a playground. "Oh, Mike! I'm so proud of you," she exclaimed. She rushed over from behind the cash register to plant a kiss on my cheek. Then realizing her commotion had caused her entire staff and a room full of diners to cease their conversations and stare at us, she pulled me front-and-center and announced, "Ladies and gentlemen, I'd like to introduce my fiancé, Lieutenant Michael Travers." As she kissed me full on the lips, the entire dining room erupted in applause.

Jodie

When Amy—my mama—come to the hospital, I thought I was still dreamin'. I take lots of naps because I got to get strong. Nurse Rebecca says I'm tired all the time because I'm growin' real fast. Well anyway, I was just wakin' up from a nap and I wasn't sure if what I was seein' was real. Lots of times in that dark room I thought I saw Mama, but it always turned out to be my 'magination. I'd rub my eyes and she'd be gone. But this time I kept rubbin' my eyes and she stayed there in the doorway lookin' pretty like I remembered her. At first, she didn't move... just stood there starin' at me like she was scared or somethin'. Then Stella took her arm and started bringing her closer to my bed real slow-like.

"Jodie, this is your mama," she said, watching me careful-like.

"Mama?" I rubbed my eyes again. I still couldn't believe she was real.

I sat up and grabbed the bedrail. Then I was on my knees and Amy rushed to me and held me tight in her arms. Yes, those were my mama's arms all right. We both started crying and rocking, rocking and crying. "Oh, Jodie, my precious Jodie," she said again and again, her arms holdin' me like they used to, like I never thought they would again. It felt so good. Now we were laughing and crying all at the same time. I rubbed her hair and patted her back. I touched her arms and held her hands to my face trying to make sure she was real. I couldn't say anything except Mama, Mama, Mama.

"I'll never leave you again, Jodie," she said. "I missed you so much. Did you feel me missin' you, Baby?" I nodded my head "yes" and hugged her some more. Then she climbed in the bed and we lay next to each other. Mama held me close for a long, long time. I don't know where Stella and Ms. Edith and Ms. Cartwright went, but they shut the door and left us alone to find our way back to each other. Mama sang to me like she used to and I fell asleep, I guess.

When Stella and Ms. Edith came back they said they had to leave for the restaurant, but Mama could eat supper with me and spend the night. I felt so happy. I wanted to show Mama the playroom and my new friend Lizzy, who I just met the day before. Lizzy can only play board games and do puzzles because she had an operation. I wanted to show Mama Nurse Rebecca and

Sadie and my tutor, Ms. Hillary, who's teaching me how to read.

"Guess what, Jodie?" Stella said. "You might be leavin' here tomorrow." Well, I started crying again when I heard that because I didn't want to leave. I was used to this place and I was afraid to leave here. Would I have to go back to that dark room and be chained to the bed with the stinky mattress? Would I be hungry and cold and lonely again?

"No, no, no! Don't wanna leave!" I cried. Mama held me and stroked my hair.

"It's okay, Baby," she said. "We're gonna be together. We'll find us a nice place to live and you can go to school and have lots of friends." Then Stella came and put her arms around both of us.

"Can Nurse Rebecca and Sadie come, too?"

"No, Sweetie," Stella said. "They have to stay here and take care of other sick kids so they can get well like you, but we can come for visits."

"But…" I started to ask if I could still play with Lizzy, but Mama interrupted me.

"I thought we might get a dog. What do you think about that, Jodie?" she asked. Well, that made my tears dry up real fast.

"A real dog?" I asked.

"A real dog. They don't allow dogs in the hospital. So, we'll have to live in a house, don't you think?"

"Okay."

"Of course, we'll have to get you some more toys, too," Stella said.

"Okay." I could tell they were trying to make me forget being sad. This here hospital was my home now. Leaving felt scary. But I sure wanted to live with Mama and Stella for always and I sure wanted a dog. Maybe it would be okay.

Then I thought of one more thing I needed to make sure of. "No Hank?" I asked.

"No Hank, Sweetie," Stella said. "Not ever again."

"Okay."

Stella

Today Amy and me—Amy and I—went to the hospital to bring Jodie home—to our temporary home, that is. Edith drove us so we could get to the restaurant in time for the lunch shift. I still can't quite believe all this is real. Edith says sometimes God works that way. We wait and wait for answers to prayer and it seems like God has deserted us, like we're alone and life is hopeless. Then, suddenly, everything falls into place. When we look back later, we can see God was workin' all along, preparin' the way—preparin' us to accept the gifts He had in store for us. I sure am grateful to Edith's God and I hope I can get some of that faith she talks about. I sure am gonna try.

When I saw Amy and Jodie holdin' each other in that hospital bed, I knew in my heart everything was gonna work out now. I'm tryin' not to have regrets. Like Dr. Morgan told me, "We can't change the past and we can't control it. But by permitting ourselves to feel the pain and deal with it, we can heal the pain. It starts by owning our own power." She keeps tellin' me it won't happen overnight. I got to be patient and I got to keep doin' the work.

It's hard not to blame myself for not gettin' Jodie and me away from Hank sooner. I feel guilty for allowin' that child to suffer all those years. I feel ashamed I didn't stand up to Hank and I feel guilty for not findin' a way to contact Amy in the prison. I remember my Mama sayin', "What don't defeat us makes us stronger." I figure Jodie and Amy and I are about as strong as any humans can be, and I'm thinkin' Edith's God might just have some special plans for our future.

A Message to My Readers

Thank you so much for reading *The Dark Room*. I hope you enjoyed it! The best way to thank an author for writing a good book is to leave an honest review. I would be grateful if you did that. Please search for my Cindy L. Freeman author page on Amazon.com and leave your review. It takes only a minute.

While the story and characters in *The Dark Room* are entirely fictitious, their development is supported by research into the complex issues of Child Abuse and Battered Woman's Syndrome. My hope for this novel is that it will touch the hearts of my readers and enlighten them about a subject that is often ignored. More importantly, I hope it will prompt victims of domestic abuse to seek empowering information and to reach out for help before it's too late. I implore you to realize that **you are not alone,** and to recognize that **the abuse is not your fault.**

If you suspect that you or someone in your life is being abused physically, verbally or emotionally, please share this book and the resources listed below.

National Center on Domestic and Sexual Violence: www.ncdsv.org. If you are not sure if you are being abused, log onto the website and refer to the Power and Control Wheel produced and distributed by NCDSV.

Free Crisis Text Line (from anywhere in the USA): 741741- a trained counselor will respond quickly.

Acknowledgments

First, I thank my Heavenly Father for the inspiration to write *The Dark Room*. In no way, do I claim to be an official emissary of divine messages. I'm not even a trained cleric. But, because *The Dark Room* appeared in my mind's eye seemingly from nowhere, I am compelled to believe the premise was inspired by the Holy Spirit.

Additionally, many human spirits have earned my gratitude for their contributions to *The Dark Room*. Since most of these associates entered my life just when I needed their friendship and expertise, I believe our resulting collaboration is nothing short of providential.

Dr. Beverly Peterson, my gifted first-reader and author of this book's Foreward, not only shared her literary expertise, but also encouraged me to keep writing when I wasn't sure I had anything new to say. As a retired English professor, she could have ripped my manuscript to shreds. Instead, she focused on the positive aspects of my writing, and, without dictating changes, showed me where I might tweak this-or-that phrase to make it clearer or more impactful. Both her friendship and her forte for written communication are treasured blessings. Thank you, Bev.

Narielle Living, my esteemed editor at High Tide Publications, excels in her editing skills because of her vast experience, but also because of her own ability to spin an impressive tale. She is an accomplished author of both fiction and non-fiction works. While Narielle never pressures me to accept her editorial suggestions, I have come to trust her wise counsel.

The providential factor in our collaboration stems from the fact that—unknown to either of us—we were doing simultaneous, but independent research on the difficult subject of Child Abuse. Narielle provided a wealth of information about the North Carolina prison system and checked the accuracy of my references to Child Protective Services. Thank you, Narielle.

For advice about legal concerns, I first consulted my dear friends, Lynda and Allan Sharrett. Allan, a retired corporate attorney, kindly scanned my work for correct terminology and basic courtroom procedures, and Lynda, an experienced non-fiction writer added a second pair of proofreading eyes. Unfortunately, Al didn't live long enough to see *The Dark Room* published, but I trust he knows how much I appreciate his generous contribution. Lynda, I thank you for your valued friendship and unwavering encouragement of my literary pursuits.

I am grateful to Dr. Suzanne Reynolds, Professor of Law and Dean of the Law School at Wake Forest University for her contribution to this labor of love. When my husband, Carl, suggested I consult his former school chum (from the first through twelfth grades), I didn't know Dr. Reynolds had been recognized by the American Bar Association for co-founding a domestic violence program that provides legal assistance to the poor. For forty-five years, Carl had regaled me with stories about his friendly academic competition with a brilliant classmate, Suzanne Reynolds. I contacted her and, after months of back-and-forth email messages, I had the genuine pleasure of finally meeting Suzanne and her attorney-husband, Robert "Hoppy" Elliot. Many people would call it "coincidence," but I recognize our connection as more evidence of providential influence. Thank you, Suzanne.

I thank Sandy Elizabeth Owens, my friend of thirty-plus years, for sharing her case-studies from eight years of working at a battered women's shelter. She was first to introduce me to the Power and Control Wheel* (see resources), and she was involved in a program designed to enlighten judges about the subject of Battered Woman Syndrome. Neither of us realized that our many casual conversations over lunch would eventually contribute to this novel. Thank you, Sandy.

As always, I am deeply grateful to my devoted husband, Carl Freeman, for his constant support and encouragement, and to Jeanne and Carl Johansen of High Tide Publications for believing enough in this aspiring writer to turn her into a published author.

Other books by Cindy L. Freeman

Unrevealed

Allison Harmon discovers that being a wealthy heiress does not guarantee a carefree life. She spends her childhood groomed by her father to take over his billion-dollar textile conglomerate. After his death, Allison is tormented by flashbacks. Convinced her family kept a secret from her, she searches for the truth. In Paris, Allison meets Jack Sanderling, an American doctoral candidate. Despite the mutual attraction, she does not divulge her identity. Jack discovers she misrepresented herself and fails to show up for their second meeting, leaving Allison heartbroken and confused. Will Allison and Jack find their way back to each other? Will Allison uncover the mystery of her childhood?

Diary in the Attic

Margaret Monroe was settling into her quiet, Friday night with a bubble bath and a glass of wine when she was interrupted by unsettling news. A cantankerous coworker, with whom she had just had an argument, had been in a devastating car accident and was calling for Margaret on her deathbed. Attending to Corrine Melton's final moments set in motion a chain of events that Margaret could have never imagined in her wildest dreams. Her reserved and standoffish coworker, who passed away that night, was accused of killing her mother, who was found dead in their home the next morning. But something about Corrine's dying words didn't quite add up.

About the Author

After forty- five years as an educator and musician, Cindy L. Freeman began writing fiction. She relishes a good mystery, as in her novella, Diary in the Attic or an intriguing family secret, as in her novel Unrevealed. In 2012, she won a contest for her essay, "A Christmas Memory" in the online publication, wydaily.com.

Cindy and her husband, Carl, live in Williamsburg, Virginia, where she has directed a music school for twenty- six years. They have two grown children and five grandchildren. You can visit her website: www.cindylfreeman.com to learn more.

"I was raised on a dairy farm in central New York," says Freeman. "Because I was allergic to everything from the cows to the crops that fed them, I spent a lot of time indoors while my siblings enjoyed farm life. I entertained myself by singing, playing the piano, and writing poetry, plays and stories. It never occurred to me that writing could become a career, especially since my heart's desire was to become a professional singer. Off I went to college to be a music major."

"As I devoted the next forty- five years to teaching and performing music—and raising a family-- my bucket list continued to include writing. I retired in 2016, and I look forward to a fulfilling second career as a novelist." Freeman's writing appeals primarily to young women in their twenties and thirties. She enjoys the creative process of analyzing her characters' motives and making them speak and act convincingly. "I like my female protagonists to come across as strong, yet vulnerable," she says.

Gloucester Library
P.O. Box 2380
Gloucester, VA 23061

Made in the USA
Middletown, DE
18 April 2017